NC

JEAN EVANS

MILLS & BOON LIMITED
ETON HOUSE 18–24 PARADISE ROAD
RICHMOND SURREY TW9 1SR

All the characters in this book have no existence outside the imagination of the Author, and have no relation whatsoever to anyone bearing the same name or names. They are not even distantly inspired by any individual known or unknown to the Author, and all the incidents are pure invention.

First published in Great Britain 1991
by Mills & Boon Limited

This edition 1991

ISBN 0 263 77282 9

Set in 11 on 12½ pt Linotron Baskerville
03-9106-45563
Typeset in Great Britain by Centracet, Cambridge
Made and printed in Great Britain

CHAPTER ONE

CRIME in Buckleigh Parva was definitely on the upturn, thought Sergeant Trevor Davis as he entered the latest report of violence into the book. 'One parrot—deceased. Said ex-parrot having expired of fright following attack, vicious and unprovoked, by one Clawdius, ginger tom, owned by Mrs Fenton-Brown of The Willows.' Trevor chewed the end of the pen. 'Mrs Fenton-Brown, in defence, insists that the said parrot provoked the said attack by the use of constant fowl language.' Chuckling, he reached for a rubber. 'Foul language, and it was her opinion that the said bird had it coming.'

A slight cough disturbed his concentrated train of thought and he half glanced up at the figure standing on the opposite side of the desk. His smile was friendly, but there was a hint of reserve in the grey-blue eyes. It was something Paula had become accustomed to.

Born and raised in a small community where everyone knew everyone else and, more to the point, took an avid interest in what everyone else was doing, she had expected it. Small communities depended upon closeness for survival.

She smiled, and the sergeant's glance deepened

into sudden interest. She was tall and slim with a cloud of dark hair framing her face. A face which Trevor, who prided himself on knowing practically everyone in the small market town, knew he couldn't possibly have forgotten if he had ever seen it before. She was wearing a dark suit, its ultra-modern elegance emphasised by the fact that its skirt stopped at knee level, revealing an attractive pair of legs in flatteringly high-heeled black shoes. She was carrying a briefcase.

Realising that he was leaning forward against the desk, Trevor straightened up and found himself gazing into a pair of eyes which were definitely more green than grey as they looked directly into his.

'Can I help you, miss?'

'As a matter of fact, I was rather hoping I could help you, Sergeant. You requested the attendance of a police surgeon. I'm Paula Fairley—Dr Fairley. What can I do for you?'

Trevor Davis gave a wide grin, showing slightly uneven teeth. 'Well, well! So you'll be with old George Reynolds, then. I heard he'd taken on a new partner.'

'Actually I'm just the locum. I joined the practice about three weeks ago. I'm covering while one of the partners is away in the States. He should be back in about three weeks' time.' Paula repeated the explanation, patiently resigned to yet another of the frequent but friendly inquisitions which had become part of her life since she had moved into the small town.

It wasn't that she minded; in fact there was something almost endearing about the amount of curiosity that had greeted her arrival in the closely-knit community. It was just that today in particular she had really hoped not to get held up. With a flu epidemic hitting just about everyone in turn, surgeries were taking even longer than usual, so that by the time she had done her calls there was barely time to get back to her room at Mrs Phillips', grab a sandwich, deal with post, take an antenatal clinic, before it was time for evening surgery.

'I hear old Doc Reynolds is thinking of retiring soon. I shouldn't wonder they'll be needing a new partner then,' Trevor remarked.

'I don't think Dr Reynolds has any firm plans.' Paula was tactfully evasive. 'He could stay for several years yet.'

'Shouldn't think it's likely, though, not with his wife been poorly and all. He must find it a bit of a struggle.'

'He hasn't actually confided in me.' Paula put her briefcase on the desk, snapped open the locks and took out a stethoscope. 'I got a message about a patient needing medical attention for a head wound. Perhaps you can fill me in on a few details and I'll take a look at him. We could start with his name.'

To her relief the sergeant lifted the desk flap and allowed her through. 'It's young Steve Watts—

local tearaway, you might say. Always in trouble of one sort or another. Started soon after he left school—couldn't get a job. I suppose he got bored.' He held open a door. 'At first it was d and ds—drunk and disorderlies. We tried a few friendly warnings, but it didn't have much effect. We picked him up a couple of times for driving under the influence. He lost his licence about twelve months ago, but it didn't stop him drinking.' He frowned. 'I thought Doc Sinclair would be over to take a look. He knows the lad—well, he should. They both grew up hereabouts.'

Paula followed along the corridor. 'Actually it's Dr Sinclair who's away.'

'Ah—well, I been away myself for a couple of weeks.'

'So you mean this Steve Watts makes a habit of this sort of thing?'

'Regular as clockwork. He's an alcoholic.'

'I see. And how old is he?'

'Twenty-four.'

Paula frowned. 'And what did you pick him up for this time?'

'The usual. He was causing a disturbance outside the local—slung a bottle through a window. Someone called us.'

'And that's when he got the head injury?'

'Not exactly.' The sergeant beckoned a young constable. 'Here, Frazer, this is Dr Fairley; she's come to take a look at Watts. Stick around just in case, will you?'

'I'm supposed to be covering the school crossing, Sarge.'

'Then get someone else to see to it, Frazer.'

'Right, Sarge.'

'Is that really necessary, Sergeant?' Paula stood back as he produced a bunch of keys, inserting one in the lock. 'I'm quite accustomed to handling patients of all types, and if you took him into custody last night. . .'

The two men exchanged a look of wry amusement. 'It'll be hours before young Steve dries out, and in the process he can get a bit nasty, especially if he's nursing the mother of all headaches.'

'Where's Dr Sinclair, then?' the younger man asked.

Paula couldn't quite suppress an illogical feeling of irritation. 'He's away in the States, attending a conference. He's due back in about three weeks.' She hadn't even met Adam Sinclair yet. How could she possibly resent a total stranger? Yet she was beginning to. In surgery the patients still asked when he was coming back, as if they tolerated her presence, in a friendly way, admittedly, but only as a final resort.

'So you'll be leaving us soon, then?'

She felt oddly gratified to hear a small note of regret in his voice. 'Not quite immediately. Not for another three weeks or so, anyway.'

'Well, that's nice, and. . .no offence.'

'None taken, but perhaps I ought to take a look at the patient, now that I'm here?'

The cell door was opened and she was immediately aware of the man lying on the bed, one arm flung over his face. He didn't move as she approached.

'Mr Watts, I'm Dr Fairley, the duty police surgeon. I understand you have a head injury?'

There was still no response from the man. Trevor Davis advanced. 'Come on now, Watts, I know you're not asleep. The lady's come specially to see you. We don't want her thinking you've got no manners, now, do we?'

Steve Watts's fist clenched, then he raised his arm, turning his head slowly to peer at Paula. 'Don't suppose you happen to have a drink?' He caught the sergeant's eye as he swung his feet down to sit, gingerly, on the bed. 'I thought not.' He rubbed a hand over his mouth and sat, head drooping, as he swayed slightly.

'The doctor wants to take a look at you, Watts.'

Paula rested her briefcase on the bed, dropped the stethoscope inside and took out an ophthalmoscope. She could see the wound on the man's forehead, where blood had congealed around a gash of about two inches in length. He jerked back, sucking in a breath as she made to touch the wound.

'It's all right, Sergeant. If I need your help I'll let you know.' She had caught Trevor Davis's wary movement out of the corner of her eye. Turning her gaze back to Steve Watts, she experienced a sense of shock as she had to remind herself that he was just two years younger than herself. He was unshaven, underweight, and looked about forty.

'I just want to examine the wound to see if it needs a few stitches.' She spoke softly to the man, ignoring the other two figures in the cell. 'I promise I'll try not to hurt you.' She showed him the ophthalmoscope. 'First I'd like to use this to take a look at your eyes. I need to see if there are any signs of concussion.'

He sat with his eyes closed, making no attempt to move as she sat beside him. She could smell the sour combination of alcohol and vomit on his clothes and wondered if he was aware of it.

'You must have quite a headache.'

'Nothing a drink wouldn't put right,' he joked feebly without looking at her.

Paula's mouth curved into an involuntary smile. 'Let me take a look at that cut, then perhaps the sergeant will see about a cup of coffee.' Her glance met the other man's, and Trevor Davis nodded briefly.

'See to it, Frazer.'

'Right, Sarge.'

'Now I just want to take a look at your eyes.' Paula was on her feet, looking down at Steve Watts. 'Can you stand?'

For a second he swayed on the edge of the bed, his hands gripping the rail as he stared at the floor. Again out of the corner of her eye she saw Trevor Davis make a move and silently signalled him to stay back. 'I want to see if he can make it by himself.'

It needed an effort, but Steve Watts was finally on his feet, swaying and pale but standing upright.

'Can you tell me how many fingers I'm holding up?'

He peered at Paula's raised hand. 'Four.'

'Good, that's fine.'

He raised a hand to his head. 'Lord, I feel lousy!'

'Sit down again.' Paula held his arm as he lowered himself on to the bed. 'How did this happen?'

He swallowed hard. 'Hit me. . .'

Paula saw Trevor Davis's expression change, sensed him tense as he shook his head. She waved him to silence. 'Hit you?'

Steve dragged the back of his hand across his mouth. 'Hit me head when I fell. Didn't feel a thing, not then. Jeez, I could do with that coffee!'

'It's on its way.' Trevor looked visibly relieved.

Paula nodded. 'I'll clean that cut up for you.' Her fingers gently probed the area, where an ugly bruise was already beginning to darken the skin. 'It looks worse than it is. You won't even need stitches—I'll use butterfly sutures to hold the edges of the skin together. Mind you, I can't promise there won't be a tiny scar.'

'I reckon I can live with that. Might even turn the girls on.'

'You could be right at that.' He was actually

quite good-looking, Paula thought. 'What about your family? Has anyone been informed?'

'There's nobody.'

'How about that wife of yours?' the sergeant intervened. 'What's her name? Sylvie?'

'Look, I said, I don't want nobody.' The response was unequivocal.

'She must be wondering where you are, lad. It can't be easy on her, not with those two kids.'

Steve Watts's mouth twisted into a line of bitterness. 'Don't you worry about Sylvie; she can look after herself. Anyway, she's gone and taken the kids with her. Probably the best thing she could have done, but I reckon she could have said where she was going.'

The older man frowned. 'You mean you don't know where she and the kids are?'

'Oh, I've got a pretty good idea. She probably thought word wouldn't get around.'

Paula got to her feet. 'Well, you'll need somewhere to go when they let you out of here.' She fastened her case and rose to her feet. 'I take it you can fix something?' She looked at Trevor Davis. 'I'm finished here. I'll leave some tablets that should fix the headache. Obviously if there's any change, any deterioration. . .'

'I'll let you know.' Trevor nodded as he went to the door. 'I'll fix something up about accommodation. Whether young Steve will appreciate it or not is another matter.'

They paused at the desk. 'I don't suppose you get much gratitude?'

He laughed. 'We don't expect it. Anyway, if past form is anything to go by, young Steve'll be out of here and away after Sylvie and the kids.'

'Do you think she'll come back to him?' Paula asked.

'No chance. Our Sylvie's got herself a boy-friend—can't say I blame her. She's never had much of a life with her old man. One of the kids ended up in hospital with a broken arm not so long ago.'

'You mean Steve did it?'

'That's what Sylvie reckoned.'

'Mm.' Paula gave him a shrewd look. 'You don't sound convinced. I think I'll have a word with social services anyway.'

'They're already on to it, through Doc Sinclair.'

'Yes, I'm sure they are. But I'm new to the area and to this particular situation.'

'And you're not convinced it's Steve's fault?'

Paula frowned. 'Are you?'

Trevor lifted the desk hatch. 'I'm a hard-bitten cynic. I never believe anything until it's proved, and even then I'm not always sure.'

Paula smiled. 'Somehow I doubt that.' She put her case down. 'Is there somewhere I can wash my hands? Then I'll give you the tablets I promised Steve. I take it you'll be releasing him?'

'As soon as he's properly sobered up.'

'Well, it won't do him any harm to sleep for the

next few hours. Get someone to keep a discreet eye on him, though. Give him a couple of tablets now, and I'd recommend that he sees his own doctor if the headache doesn't clear within twenty-four hours.'

'Don't worry, I'll see to it that he gets the message. There's a cloakroom just down the corridor there—help yourself. Fancy a cup of tea before you leave?'

'I'd love one.' Paula smiled ruefully. 'I missed my morning break, but surgery seemed to go on for ever.'

'And we called you out here.'

'It's all part of the job. The trouble is I had a list of visits as long as your arm and I'm still trying to find my way around, which is why I took so long getting here, and I'm not finished yet. So I'd better skip the tea. The Cooper boys have all got measles, from the sound of things.'

'Sounds about right,' Trevor chuckled. 'They always do everything in threes, including getting stuck up a tree. Still, if it's any consolation, you're not doing so bad, and this wasn't exactly an emergency.' He reached for a file. 'Perhaps you'd like to go out for a bite of lunch one day, when you're free. The local pub does a pretty good range of food. If you're not otherwise engaged, that is? I could introduce you to a few of the local farmers.' He gave an embarrassed grin.

'I'd like that. Perhaps I can let you know when I'm free. But right now I'd better get cleaned up and make a move before my patients start ringing the surgery to complain.'

'I don't suppose you're finding it easy with Doc Sinclair away?'

'You noticed!' She laughed wryly. 'If one more person asks when he's due back I may scream!'

'Don't let it get you down. He's a good bloke. Most of the folk around here have known him since he was a kid.'

Paula smiled. 'I'm relieved to hear it. I was beginning to think he was some sort of paragon, not quite human.'

'Oh, there's nothing wrong with Adam. He just takes a bit of getting to know, that's all.'

'Unfortunately I'm not going to have time to do that. By the time he comes back I shall be just about due to leave. Anyway, I really must clean up and be on my way before someone decides to send out a search party.'

'I'll give the surgery a ring if you like. Let them know roughly when you expect to be back.'

'Would you?' She smiled her relief before heading for the cloakroom, praying there wouldn't be any further calls to add to the list. She had missed her coffee break and her stomach was beginning to give discernible reminders that it would soon be lunchtime.

She emerged minutes later to find Trevor Davis engaged in conversation with another man who was leaning across the desk. Paula's cursory glance took in jeans-clad legs, a soft leather jacket and dark, rain-dampened hair—or was it snow?

Neither man was aware of her presence as her troubled gaze went briefly to the window, where her worst fears were confirmed. It was snow, and it was coming down quite heavily. She sighed heavily, wondering if spring was ever going to put in an appearance. Accustomed to Hampshire's gentler seasons as she was, the lingering ferocity of a Midlands winter had come as something of a shock. That's all I need, she thought, wondering briefly what the odds were on getting back before the rapidly fading daylight closed in.

She would write out the prescription and leave a note rather than interrupt the conversation going on at the desk. She bent to retrieve her briefcase from where she had left it by the door and took out her prescription pad.

She wasn't sure when it was that the men's conversation began to intrude upon her consciousness, or perhaps it was simply that the tall figure standing with his back to her straightened suddenly, giving her an impression of tanned, chiselled features and blue eyes as he stared past her at the snow falling against the window before his gaze passed briefly over her with a smile of polite interest, taking in the small oval of her face, the fall of thick dark hair as she bent over the prescription pad, embarrassed at having been caught staring.

'Bit of a change, this must be,' the sergeant was saying.

The man gave a deep-throated laugh. 'You could say. Typical British weather!'

'I heard you were away for another three or four weeks.'

'That's right, I was. The idea was that I'd stay on with a colleague in the States after the conference had ended. It was going to be partly holiday, partly a fact-finding tour, but his father died suddenly and I decided my presence would be a bit surplus to requirements, so I decided to head for home. I can't say I'm sorry. America's a great place, but it's big and noisy; not everyone's cup of tea. Certainly not mine, so I caught the first available plane, landed a couple of hours ago and decided to phone the practice, just to let them know I was back and available if required.'

'I dare say they were glad. This must be a busy time of year for you.'

'You could say. Anyway, they mentioned that you had a spot of bother over here, so I dropped in on my way. I gather they've taken on a locum, some youngster, Paul someone—it was a bad line. He's probably still wet behind the ears, but I don't suppose they were exactly spoilt for choice. Not many GPs want to leave the big city for a spell of rural isolation—at least, that's how most of them see it up here. I can only think this one must have been desperate.'

Paula found herself listening, the colour flooding into her cheeks as a growing realisation dawned. Surely it couldn't be, and yet. . .

'So you haven't met this locum yet, then?'

'No. I left it to George and Bill to fix something if they felt it was necessary—after all, they were the ones who were going to have to work with whoever they chose. As it is, even with me back earlier than intended, we're probably going to be glad of the extra cover for the next few weeks. I hear you've been having a flu epidemic over here.' He grinned. 'With our luck the new bloke will just be finding his way around when it's time to leave.'

Paula's gaze locked with the embarrassed stare of Trevor Davis as he seemed suddenly to become aware of her presence.

'Er. . . I think perhaps there's someone here you should meet, Doc.'

Paula's heels clicked across the floor as, restraining her anger, she swept up the prescription she had written out and carried it towards the desk. 'I'll leave this with you, Sergeant. I've written a note since I don't have time to stop and explain. I'd hate to have anyone think I'd been deliberately wasting time.'

The man turned his gaze full on her now. He was taller than she had first imagined and his eyes held a glint of appreciation as he straightened up.

'You must be new around here—I reckon to know most faces. Adam Sinclair.' He proffered his hand, studying her with the kind of cool speculation that made her feel oddly vulnerable. She wondered briefly whether her chances of future employment would be seriously prejudiced is she were to land a slap firmly across the arrogant features, then thought better of it.

'Paula Fairley.' Her smile was rigid with suppressed fury and, just for a moment, she thought she detected a slight drawing together of his dark brows.

'Staying or just visiting?'

'Staying, for a while anyway.'

'Well, in that case we may meet again.'

Her teeth grated on a smile. 'Oh, I should think there's a distinct possibility we'll be seeing quite a lot of each other, Doctor. Though from the sound of things I imagine you must be kept pretty busy, running a large practice virtually single-handed.'

Trevor Davis made a slight choking sound in his throat.

Smiling sweetly, Paula released her hand from Adam Sinclair's firm grip and reached for her briefcase. 'Well, if there's nothing else, Sergeant, I'd better get on. I mustn't take all day. I still have a couple of calls to make and, being still wet behind the ears, who knows how long that may take?'

Without waiting to see the effect her words had had, she turned on her heel and walked away, but not before she had heard the swift intake of Adam Sinclair's breath, seen the swift narrowing of his eyes. Perhaps she had gone a little over the top. She was, after all, going to have to work with this man for the next few weeks at least.

Her mouth tightened. She might have to work with him, but she didn't have to like him, and, anyway, what was three weeks? Surely she could work with her worst enemy for that long? So what was it about Adam Sinclair that was making her so irrationally edgy?

Her shoes made light imprints in the snow as she walked to her car, fumbled with the key before actually finding the ignition and, conscious of the figure of Adam Sinclair reflected in the driving mirror, drove away.

CHAPTER TWO

'THERE we are, then, Mrs Hardcastle.' Paula wrote out a prescription, handing it to the woman seated opposite. 'Take one tablet three times a day, after meals, and I'm sure you'll soon be feeling much better. If in about ten days you find the cough hasn't cleared, then come back and we'll arrange a chest X-ray, but I'm sure it won't come to that. You were wise to come when you did.'

Mrs Hardcastle got to her feet, clutching the prescription with a smile of relief. 'I'm glad I wasn't wasting your time. I know how hard you doctors work, out all hours and in all weathers, especially this time of the year.'

'Don't worry about it.' Paula smiled as she escorted the woman to the door. 'That's what we're here for, and I'll pop out to see your husband in a couple of days. The district nurse tells me his leg is healing nicely.'

'That's right, so it is, thanks to young Dr Sinclair.'

It was a sentiment echoed by so many patients that Paula returned to her desk battling against a totally alien feeling of depression. Sooner or later she knew she was going to have to come face to face again with Adam Sinclair, and it wasn't a meeting she relished, after her encounter with him the previous day.

Luckily he hadn't put in an appearance for the evening surgery. Not that it had been necessary for him to do so. Now that the recent flu epidemic seemed to have run its course she and Bill Patterson were finally beginning to see a lessening of calls for visits as well as in the number of patients coming to the surgery, and, Paula had to admit, it was a relief. As a medical student she had become used to long spells on duty with little or no sleep, but since she had qualified it was surprising how quickly she had forgotten what it was like to be woken from a deep sleep and having to stumble out of bed. You're out of condition, that's the trouble with you, she told herself firmly, reaching for the buff-coloured files on her desk.

She had just seen the last patient of the morning and was looking forward to her coffee when someone tapped at the door and came in without waiting for her to respond.

Paula frowned. Gill Cleaver in Reception had said there were no more patients. Perhaps she had somehow managed to miss one of the cards. Her frown deepened then as she looked up and saw Adam Sinclair. His gaze was directed, frowning, from her open briefcase to her face, and she found herself thinking that he looked quite different, quite good-looking even in a rugged sort of way. It might have been the fact that he had had a shave, or the fact that he was wearing a dark suit instead of the faded jeans. There were tiny lines of fatigue round his eyes, but he seemed younger than she had first thought; probably around thirty-five, she guessed.

Absorbed in her critical survey, she suddenly became aware that his own deep-set blue eyes were appraising her in return. It was a disconcerting feeling, as if she were being examined minutely under a microscope. Illogically, it made her want to check that her mascara hadn't run or that a wisp of hair hadn't escaped from its restraining clip. She resisted the urge. Instead she moved to stand behind her desk.

'Can I help you, Doctor? I'm still rather busy.' She made an exaggerated play of shuffling the pile of case-notes, and was relieved when the telephone rang. But any hopes she might have entertained that he would simply turn and leave seemed doomed to disappointment. He remained, stoically gazing round the small surgery as she dealt with a patient's query.

When finally she put the phone down, Adam Sinclair was standing with his hands in his pockets, staring up at a small watercolour painting on the wall. The stance seemed to emphasise the power in the shoulders beneath the jacket.

'It's nice.' He nodded towards the painting.

Unable to resist the temptation, she straightened the frame. 'I like it.'

'I don't recognise the scene.'

'You wouldn't. It was painted quite close to where my father lives. . .lived.'

'Ah, that explains it. I knew it couldn't be anywhere local.' Adam gave her a searching look. 'I heard he died fairly recently.'

Paula had to stifle a sudden and totally illogical feeling that his presence somehow made the room seem smaller. 'That's right.' She nodded. 'Twelve months ago, actually.'

'I gather he'd been ill for some time and that you'd been looking after him. You must have found that quite a tie.'

'Not at all,' she dismissed coolly, wondering just how much information about her personal life this man had managed to acquire in so short a space of time. 'He'd had a stroke, and it left him partially paralysed—not so much that he couldn't do anything. In any case, he was always far too independent a spirit to welcome having everything done for him. But he needed help.'

'And you just happened to be there.'

'I *chose* to be there.'

'Even so, you must have been glad to get back to work.'

Paula looked at him sharply. Was he implying that she had been lucky to find a practice desperate enough to take her, or was she being over-sensitive? In a way it was probably true, she acknowledged ruefully. Her father's illness had changed a lot of things, including her plans. Selling the cottage had become a nightmare. It might once have been a buyer's dream, but that had been a long time ago. By the time she had found someone prepared to take on the task of an almost total renovation, there had been little left to recompense her for the months of not working—certainly nothing for luxuries. She had been lucky to inherit an almost new car. That at least had been a godsend.

She sighed, brushing back a strand of hair. 'I suppose I was relieved, if I'm honest. I'd only recently qualified when he had his stroke.' She broke off, wondering why it was that she suddenly seemed to be defending herself to a stranger. After all, it was nothing to Adam Sinclair that she had stayed at home because her father had refused to have a nurse. After years—a lifetime—of caring for other people she understood that he found it hard to accept a sudden almost total dependence upon someone else. All right, so she had lied a little. Her father had been more than slightly disabled by his stroke, but far worse than any disability was the fact that he had seemed to choose not to help himself. Instead of fighting he had become first resentful, then angry, and with the anger had come selfishness.

Paula sighed without realising that she did so. Small wonder that Ralph had grown tired of waiting for her to be available! What with the hours she worked as well as looking after her father, there was precious little time for anything or anyone else. Perhaps the decision to end their engagement had been for the best. At the time she had told herself that tiredness was responsible for her lack of reaction when Ralph had suggested they might both be better off if they were free to go their own way. What he meant, of course, was that *he* would be free. She couldn't blame him, hadn't grieved either, not even when, a month later, she heard that he was engaged to someone else.

She frowned. 'Look, I really am busy. Did you want to see me for anything important? Only I've got a list of calls.' She glanced at her watch, hoping he would get the message.

'The name's Adam.'

She reached for her coat and was struggling into it when its weight was lifted from her. Her body brushed against his, sending a crazy shock wave running through her. Startled, she glanced involuntarily up at him. 'I can manage, thanks, and I think I prefer formality, while we're on duty at least, if you don't mind.'

Blue eyes regarded her with an unreadable expression. Only the slight tremor at the corner of his mouth suggested that he was amused. 'Are you always so independent?'

The words were so softly spoken that she wasn't even sure she had heard them. 'I beg your pardon?'

'I said are you always so formal? Do you insist on calling Bill Patterson Doctor?'

'Well, no.'

'Or George?' Adam Sinclair challenged softly.

'That's different,' she snapped, moving away from him.

His dark brows drew together. 'You mean I have to apply for a special dispensation?'

Now she knew he was laughing at her, and for some reason she felt herself respond with a faint smile. Perhaps she was being a little childish, bearing a grudge towards someone who, after all, knew nothing about her, or her capabilities as a doctor.

'I've had a chance to get to know them,' she explained. 'I've already begun to think of them as friends.'

'And I'm the enemy,' came the quiet reply. 'I do seem to have the knack of offending you, don't I?'

Suddenly Paula felt herself blushing. 'I wouldn't put it quite like that.' She waited for him to move so that she could get to the door, but he remained impassively blocking her way.

'I can explain,' he began.

'There's really no need,' she countered briskly. 'It's really not that important. We got off to a bad start; let's just leave it at that.'

'But I think there's a very good reason why we should clear this up. Patients can be surprisingly receptive to any hint of strained relationships between members of the practice, so if we're going to work together for the next few weeks at least we're going to have to call some sort of truce.'

Did he have to make it quite so clear that as far as he was concerned he was only tolerating her presence for as long as was absolutely necessary? Paula drew herself up to her full five feet eight inches and still had to look up at the man towering above her. 'I think I can be relied upon to behave in a professional manner.'

'But not too stiff and starchy, I trust. We don't want to frighten the patients away.'

She looked at him sharply, the gently mocking words completely taking the wind out of her sails, and, almost in spite of herself, she heard herself laugh.

'I promise not to pin up posters saying "Dr Sinclair is bad for your health". Will that do?'

His mouth twisted. 'It's not exactly what I had in mind, but it will do for a start.' He sobered. 'The truth is that when we first met I was suffering badly from jet lag. I missed a flight, which meant I spent hours hanging around the airport before I could get another. It was entirely my own fault, because I hadn't made a booking.' He raked a hand through his dark hair. 'Suddenly it all seemed to catch up. The conference went well, but it was two weeks virtually non-stop. I don't know how the Americans do it, but they seemed to have far more energy than I had! By the end of it I was looking forward to a break—then Larry's father died suddenly.' He frowned. 'I could have stayed on, I was asked to, but I would have felt like an intruder. Can you understand that?'

Paula nodded. 'I think so. A family needs to be together at a time like that.'

'That's what I figured. Besides, ridiculous as it may seem, I was glad to be back.'

Frustratingly, Paula found herself wondering if

he was married. She swallowed hard, telling herself that she wasn't interested in Adam Sinclair's personal life one way or the other. 'I can quite easily believe it,' she said flatly. 'Don't most people prefer to be with the things and people they care about?'

An enigmatic expression she couldn't fathom lurked in his eyes. 'Not everyone shares your view.'

Something in the way he uttered the cryptic words made her wonder briefly what lay behind them, but her curiosity was left unsatisfied as he went on.

'The minute I stepped off the plane this end the first thing I did was to ring the practice from the airport. I wanted to get back to work. I thought I might be needed.'

'Surely you must have known they'd taken on a locum to cover while you were away?'

His dark brows drew together. 'Ordinarily, yes, but as it happens I was asked to stand in at the conference at the last minute when the original lecturer was taken ill. We'd worked together in the past, so I knew the groundwork. It all happened in a bit of a rush. George said they'd cover somehow. He told me just to pack and go. I'd forgotten all about the possibility of a locum until Mrs Cleaver reminded me when I phoned in. It was then she told me about Stevie Watts.'

'And also the point at which you made the assumption that I was probably still too wet behind the ears to handle the situation.' She couldn't resist the gibe, and saw him wince as it hit home.

'The thought did cross my mind.'

'It seemed to make it all the way to your mouth as well.'

His eyes narrowed. '*Touché!* The truth is. . .well, you could say I have a personal interest where Steve is concerned. I've spent the past six months trying to keep him out of prison.'

'I rather got the impression from Sergeant Davis that you could be fighting a losing battle.'

'I don't give up that easily,' he said with narrowed eyes. 'Deep down he's not a bad kid. He just has a few problems—usually alcohol-related. I take it that's what was at the root of this latest flare-up?'

Paula frowned. 'I rather gather it was something different this time. Oh, he'd been drinking, but there was a fight, something to do with his wife. . . Sylvie? I understand she's left him and taken the children.'

Adam swore softly. 'I might have known Sylvie would be at the bottom of it one way or another! She usually is. Heaven knows, he'd have been better off if he'd never met her, let alone married her.'

'They may not agree,' Paula said sharply. 'What about the children?'

'What about them?' Adam said drily. 'There's no guarantee they're even his.'

Paula swallowed hard. 'I see.' She looked up to see him regarding her with cynical amusement.

'Most people may have Steve down as a hard-case, but he's surprisingly old-fashioned in some ways. Sylvie got pregnant, not for the first time, but this time she found someone who was sucker enough to want to marry her, to try to give her and the twins a home. Of course, it didn't really stand a chance. Sylvie was never a one-man woman. He knew that, but I think he hoped he could make it work.'

Paula hesitated, then said slowly, 'I can see why you might have resented my being there.'

'It wasn't exactly resentment. It certainly doesn't excuse the things I said.'

He was probably right, Paula thought with a flash of the same irrational irritation she'd felt before. So why was *she* suddenly feeling guilty? 'Well, now that you're back surely you don't have to get straight back to work? I thought you were due some time off.'

'I suppose I am.'

'Then why not take a holiday anyway?'

His eyes narrowed to glittering blue slits. 'If you go on at this rate I may begin to get the idea I'm dispensable!'

Paula felt herself blush. 'That wasn't exactly what I meant. I just thought that as I'm here anyway. . .'

'I can safely take myself off and leave the reins in your capable hands.'

Her eyes flashed. 'You seem determined to put the wrong interpretation on my words! Tell me, is it locums in general you have something against, or me in particular, because if it's the fact that I'm a woman——'

He laughed aloud. 'Oh, not that old chestnut! I have no objection to you at all, and most certainly not as a woman.'

Paula's gaze flew up to meet his and found his eyes regarding her with mocking amusement. Her cheeks flamed. 'Then perhaps you doubt my qualifications?'

'Are you always so quick to jump to conclusions?'

'I don't see what other conclusions I'm supposed to draw. I don't have to stay. Now that you're back I can easily leave. . .'

She was heading for the door when his hand caught her arm and he swung her to face him. She was suddenly conscious of a crazy vortex of emotions that surged over her like a huge tidal wave as she looked up into the steely blue eyes and saw his mouth curve in silent laughter.

'Are you always this fiery?'

'Only when provoked.' Furiously she tried to free her arm, but his grasp merely tightened, drawing her inexorably closer.

'I do seem to bring out the worst in you, don't I?' He didn't wait for a reply. Instead his mouth tightened. 'The truth is, you came as something of a surprise.'

'You mean a blow to your ego!'

'You could say.' His mouth twisted into a wry grin before sobering again. 'The truth is I'd convinced myself that I was the best person, the only person to sort Steve Watts out.'

'Do you always take on the role of counsellor, Doctor?'

'Only if I can't avoid it.' Humour lurked in his thickly lashed eyes. 'So, what are you going to do when your time with us is up?'

Paula blinked hard. 'Do?'

His eyes were dark as he looked down at her. 'I take it you have plans?'

She swallowed hard. 'I hadn't actually thought that far ahead.' She frowned. 'I suppose I should——' She broke off as a light tapping came at the door before it swung open and George Reynolds, the senior partner, popped his head round.

'Ah, glad I caught you both. Patients all gone?'

'Just,' Paula confirmed. Her breathing became more even as she found herself released. 'I've a house call to make.'

'Urgent?'

'Well,' she looked at the card, purposely avoiding Adam Sinclair's gaze, 'no, actually. Mrs Briggs, a more or less routine visit and a top-up prescription for her arthritis pills.'

'Good. In that case could you both spare five minutes to pop into my office? Just something I'd like to get sorted out while we're all here.'

Following George, Paula realised he hadn't actually asked Adam if he were free for the impromptu meeting. She glanced up at him as he held the door open for her to pass. His enigmatic features revealed nothing. Only now, as she stepped into George's office, did it occur to her that perhaps she had completely misread the motive behind his questioning.

How stupid of her! She felt the colour steal warmly into her cheeks. Of course her job as locum had only been necessary while Adam Sinclair was away. His early return had put a very different reflection on things. For a start, it meant she was no longer needed.

'Make yourselves comfortable.' George waved them both to seats, poured coffee and handed them both a cup. 'Bill's already out on a call, but it doesn't matter—he knows what I'm about to say.' He returned to his own seat behind the desk from where he studied Paula. 'The thing is, we wondered whether you might be prepared to stay on as locum for a while longer?'

She stared at him, coffee-cup halfway to her mouth. 'You want me to stay? But. . .'

'Yes, I know it's probably very inconvenient. You may have other plans.'

'No. No, it's not that.' Her startled gaze flew to Adam Sinclair. His attention seemed to be focused studiously on the plate of biscuits. 'I. . .er. . .how long did you have in mind?'

'Three months, if you could manage it.'

'But I thought once Dr. . .once Adam got back. . .'

'I know,' George conceded. 'It's entirely my fault—I've put you in a difficult position. The thing is, Bill is still due some leave, and I'd quite like to take a couple of weeks myself fairly soon.' He put his cup down, pushing it to one side. 'The thing is, I'd really like to spend a little more time with Margaret.'

Adam's eyes narrowed as he looked at the older man. 'Are you worried about her, George?'

'No, no, not really. It's just that she's not been too well lately, and I feel she'd like me to be there.' The phone rang in the adjoining office, and George got to his feet, excusing himself as he went to answer it. 'I've been expecting a call. Talk among yourselves; I'll be back in a minute.'

Paula looked at Adam. 'Perhaps it's this flu that's going around. We're getting more cases every day.'

Adam stirred sugar into his second cup of coffee. 'Have you met Margaret?'

'Only very briefly, when I first arrived, but not since. She seemed very nice.'

'Margaret *is* nice. She doesn't go out a great deal.'

'Oh?'

He looked down at her from where he stood by the window. 'She has MS—multiple sclerosis. It was diagnosed several years ago. In fact she's one of the luckier ones in that her symptoms have been relatively mild, until now.' He frowned. 'It was always on the cards, of course, that she might get worse. I know some don't, or they can have remissions lasting for years.'

Paula put her own cup down and stood up. 'I had no idea. She wasn't in a wheelchair.'

'No, that's a fairly recent development.'

'I can see why George is worried.'

'He thinks the world of her. It's a pretty rare thing these days to find a perfectly happy marriage.'

Again there was a note of cynicism in his voice, or had she imagined it? There was no way to find out, as George bustled back into the room, his greying hair ruffled.

'Had to arrange some urgent X-rays for a patient. So. . .' he looked at Paula '. . .the question is, do you think you could bear with us for a while longer? You've settled in well. I don't have to tell you that the patients have taken to you, which is half the battle, and it goes without saying that it would be much appreciated by all concerned if you could help out.'

Paula felt her gaze drawn involuntarily to Adam Sinclair as he stood at the window, but his back was to her, denying her any glimpse of his expression. Studying the back of the dark head, she wondered whether he would endorse that vote of confidence. More to the point, how did she feel about the possibility of working with *him* for the next three months?

He turned slowly and she could feel the blue eyes studying her without giving any hint in return of what he was thinking.

She drew a breath. 'I'd be happy to help out. As it happens, I don't have any other plans.'

'Well, that's marvellous! So it's all settled, then.'

Paula couldn't resist meeting Adam Sinclair's gaze challengingly. She resigned herself to seeing disappointment etched into the handsome features, but instead she was almost certain she detected a hint of a smile.

'Welcome to the firm,' he said softly.

She offered him a reluctant grin of her own. 'It's only temporary,' she reminded him.

'I think I can stand it if you can.'

It wasn't until later that she began to think seriously about what she had taken on. She didn't know anything about Adam Sinclair except that he was right; he did seem to have the ability to provoke a great many conflicting emotions in her, none of which was going to make for an easy working relationship. But then, she told herself firmly, it was only for three months, not a lifetime. Surely she could survive that?

CHAPTER THREE

'You must have known before we went in that he was going to ask me to stay on.' Humour took the edge off the faintly accusatory note in her voice as Paula faced Adam Sinclair in the corridor.

'Not exactly.' He went ahead of her to the now empty waiting-room, peering at the list of messages left on the Reception desk. 'George talked vaguely about it this morning when I first came in. Damn!' He frowned at the piece of paper before shoving it unceremoniously into his jacket pocket. 'I'm supposed to be at a meeting. . . It was my first chance to talk to him about Margaret—which reminds me, I must go and see her.' He studied her as if regathering his thoughts. 'It wasn't an official practice meeting, otherwise you'd have been invited, of course.'

'Of course.' Paula gave him a solemn look. She wondered if he knew that the collar of his shirt was slightly frayed or that his jacket had seen better days. She gave herself a mental shake, bringing her attention back to what he was saying.

'I know Bill's been hoping to fit in some leave for ages, and as you hadn't actually made any plans it seemed the ideal solution.'

'But you didn't know then that I hadn't made any plans.'

Blue eyes met hers. 'Well, let's say I was hoping. You mentioned to George when you first arrived that you hadn't had time to fix anything too definite, so,' a faint smile twisted the corners of his mouth, 'someone else's loss is our gain, for the next three months anyway.'

The genuine note of pleasure in his voice sent a tiny and thoroughly illogical *frisson* of happiness running through her, and she felt the faint tide of colour swim into her face as she sent him an answering smile. 'I've enjoyed being here. It's a beautiful area, and the people are friendly. Everyone has made me feel welcome.'

'We aim to please.' His gaze levelled with hers before he frowned at his watch. 'I have to admit I can see the sense in having a female doctor in the practice. Some of our patients prefer to be given a choice. This way at least we should get some interesting feedback. Who knows?' He reached for his briefcase and car keys. 'You could be setting a precedent. I'd better get going. Judging from this list I get the distinct feeling all my house calls have been mounting up while I've been away.'

'It must be nice to be so popular.' Paula grinned, and had half turned away when the pile of case-notes began to slide from her fingers, crashing to the floor and scattering in all directions. Annoyed with her own carelessness, she bent quickly to retrieve them just as he followed suit. Their bodies collided, momentarily knocking the breath out of her. She rocked backwards, and instinctively he reached out, grasping her upper arms and drawing her towards him as he straightened up.

'Here, you'd better let me.' In one fluid movement he swept up the cards and placed them in her hands.

Paula felt the breath catch in her throat as a feeling of physical awareness swept through her, then she pulled her hands out of his grasp. 'Thanks.'

'Think nothing of it.' His gaze narrowed briefly. 'I'll see you in the morning.'

She nodded. Watching the door close behind him, she felt the first tiny feeling of pleasure fade. For a few moments there, she had actually imagined he was welcoming her on a personal level. On reflection she decided that Adam Sinclair was simply pleased to have found a way of easing his own case-load. But then wasn't that precisely the reason she was here?

It was evening and dark by the time she had finished her visits and finally returned to the tiny flat she had managed to rent for what was to have been a brief stay in the town.

Letting herself in through the front door, she instantly began switching on all the lights and put a tape into the small radio-cassette. Anything to make things a little more welcoming. Not that the rooms were unpleasant; on the contrary they were clean and comfortable, if sparsely furnished. What they lacked, she decided, was those little human touches that made a home. On the other hand, it hadn't seemed too bad when she had known it was only going to be for a matter of weeks, but now that things had changed. . . She sighed. I'll have to start looking for something else, something with a little more space, she told herself as she showered and slipped into a warm towelling robe. I'll start looking tomorrow, or maybe at the weekend.

She felt exhausted as she padded over to light the gas fire and then into the kitchen to switch on the kettle before gazing optimistically into the fridge, trying to decide what to eat. Finally settling for cheese on toast and a cup of coffee, she carried it on a tray into the small sitting-room, where she made a perfunctory attempt at eating before opening the day's mail.

Two bills, one reminder that a magazine subscription was now overdue and a letter from Ralph. She was vaguely surprised to see his familiar handwriting on the envelope. They hadn't corresponded for some time. There hadn't been any reason to keep in touch, especially after he had become engaged, but it was good to know that at least they had parted amicably, as friends.

She purposely kept his letter till last. Sinking back into the ancient, chintz-covered armchair, she slit the envelope. The words leapt out at her from the page.

> I know you'll be pleased to hear that Pam and I are getting married next month. It's all been fairly sudden; we hadn't planned for it to

happen quite this fast. The thing is, I've been offered a job overseas and I've decided to accept. Pam is all for it. Anyway, I wanted you to know, and this letter is by way of an invitation to the wedding. You know you're welcome, and we'd both like to take the opportunity to say goodbye to all our friends. So, if there's a chance, do make it. . .

Paula let the hand holding the letter fall and was surprised to feel it shaking slightly. Ralph—getting married! She was glad, of course she was. She liked Pam. They made an ideal couple. But it might have been you, if things had been different, the thought flashed into her mind, and was dismissed instantly. She hadn't been in love with Ralph, nor, if the truth were known, had he been in love with her; it was as simple as that. Looking back, she could see it had never been the kind of relationship that would set the world on fire. Or had she perhaps expected too much?

She was sitting frowning into the artificial flicker of the gas fire. Surely before you could set the world alight there had to be some kind of spark between two people, some irresistible attraction? What did it take to make it happen? More to the point, what happened when it did?

Paula was taken unawares as a fleeting but none the less disturbing image of Adam Sinclair's attractive features flashed completely unbidden into her mind, and she wondered what it would be like to be married to such a man.

She shook herself. What on earth was she doing, daydreaming about a man she hardly even knew? She rose quickly to her feet on the surprisingly uncomfortable thought that he might be married anyway.

She was huddled on the settee, sipping at a cup of hot chocolate and trying to stifle a yawn as she watched the late news on television, when the phone rang. Groaning, she eased her legs out from under her. 'Oh, no! Please don't be an emergency, not now!' Fumbling for the phone, she ran a hand through her hair. 'Dr Fairley speaking.'

There was a moment's hesitation before a voice which was fast becoming familiar spoke in her ear. 'Adam here—Adam Sinclair.'

Paula felt her heart miss a beat. Instinctively her hand drew the sash around the waist of her towelling robe tighter before she chided herself for the gesture. It wasn't as if he could see her in her state of undress. 'Oh. . .er. . .yes, hello.'

'I hope I didn't disturb you.'

More than he could know, she thought wildly. Reaching for her watch, she peered at the small dial. Eleven-thirty. So what time did he go to bed? Or perhaps he'd been out for the evening.

'No, not at all.'

His voice sounded a little strained. 'I've been working on a paper I'm supposed to be writing for a journal and I've only just realised how late it is. You were probably asleep.'

'As a matter of fact I was watching television.'

'In that case I hope I'm not interrupting anything too exciting.'

Not much danger of that, unless you count the fact that I'm half naked and snuggled up to a cup of hot chocolate! She gave an involuntary laugh, turning it into a cough. 'I was just cursing. I was thinking of going to bed when the phone rang. I thought it was a patient.'

'That's why I'm calling. I should have told you earlier, but it went clean out of my head, then I missed you when you went back to the surgery. I meant to say that I'll take over the emergency calls tonight and for the rest of the week.'

'There's really no need——'

'I'd say there is,' came the quiet rejoinder. 'You covered for me while I was away.'

'I was under the impression that was what I was here for, and I like to earn my keep.'

They both laughed, then there was an awkward silence.

'Yes, well, now I'm back I reckon it's time I took a turn. I like to earn my keep too. Besides, I don't want people getting the idea that I'm dispensable.'

Fat chance of that happening, Paula thought. 'But you must still be suffering from jet lag.'

'Surprisingly I feel fine. By tomorrow it may be a different story, of course, but it's time I got back into the routine.'

'Well, in that case, I can certainly do with the beauty sleep.'

'I hadn't noticed anything wrong with the way you look.' There was a moment's pause, then his voice came back with an added note of briskness. 'So it's settled, then. I'll get any calls directed to me—and now I'd better get back to this paper. I'll probably see you in the morning.'

'Yes, of course.' But the receiver had already clicked and she knew he hadn't even heard. The small room seemed suddenly very empty as she replaced the receiver.

In fact she didn't see any of the partners until late the following morning. It was raining as she hurried into the surgery, stopping briefly at the Reception desk.

Mrs Cleaver handed her a bundle of letters and nodded ruefully in the direction of the waiting-room. 'It's pretty full in there, I'm afraid.'

'Oh, lord! Have the others started yet?'

'Only Dr Sinclair, but he came in early.' Gill Cleaver smiled. 'Don't worry about it. Your being here is a bonus. I only wish we had the permanent luxury of an extra doctor. It would lighten the load for all of us, including the patients. I'm afraid now that Adam is back you'll have to use the small consulting-room at the end of the corridor. It's really only a treatment-room. . .'

'I'm sure it will be fine.' Paula waved, heading for the door. 'I'll manage. From the look of things out there I'd better get started.' Not that she was likely to be inundated with pleas for her services, she thought, now that the beloved Dr Adam was back. The tiny feeling of depression hovered like a small black cloud as she shed her coat, checking her appearance in the long mirror before ringing for her first patient. Fashionable knee-length straight skirt, cashmere sweater in a vivid jade green, a light, Italian-style scarf draped softly around her neck and shoulders. Was the skirt perhaps a shade too short? Even if it was—not that she had ever received any complaints—it was a little late to do anything about it now.

Paula seated herself at the desk, hitched the skirt into place and jabbed her hand down on the bell.

Contrary to all expectations, she was kept surprisingly busy, and it was a relief when she saw her last patient of the morning out and was finally free to take a coffee break. Wandering into the small room provided for this purpose, as well as the occasional practice meeting, she realised she wasn't the first to make her escape. Bill Patterson was already helping himself to coffee from the Thermos jugs which had been left ready on a tray. He looked up as Paula entered—forty years old, tall, good-looking, white teeth flashing a smile of welcome.

'Ah, the hordes are about to descend, and here was I thinking I'd get first go at the chocolate biscuits. Coffee?'

'Oh, yes, please. The biscuits are all yours, but

coffee I must have before I can even think of setting foot outside.'

'I know the feeling.' Bill handed her a cup. 'I heard the good news, by the way. You've decided to stay on.'

'For a while anyway. It was no hardship,' Paula confessed. 'I hadn't any other pressing commitments.'

'Well, I'm delighted. It makes a change to see a pretty face around the place—brightens things up. Apart from which, some of our female patients will be pleased. It's natural enough that some of them prefer to see a lady doctor.' He eyed the biscuits. 'Got many visits?'

'Enough!'

'It'll get easier,' he promised, 'once the bad weather lets up and people start to get over the post-Christmas blues.' He turned away from the window.

Seeing the smile, which didn't quite reach the tired brown eyes, Paula was emboldened to ask, 'Was that a generalisation or speaking personally?'

Her shrewdness seemed to startle him. 'Goodness, do I look that bad?'

'Well, a shade jaded, maybe.' She chuckled wryly. 'Aren't you due for some holidays?'

'Overdue, actually.' Bill poured a second cup of coffee. 'It's not easy trying to find dates that are compatible with my work and Louise's job at the bank.' A tiny frown etched its way between his brows.

'Ah, yes, you mentioned that she works for one of the local branches.'

Bill half sat, half leaned against the table. 'She's the branch manager, to be more precise, and damn good at her job.'

'You must be very proud of her.'

'Of course.' His glance edged up to lock with hers. Paula told herself she had imagined the faint trace of bitterness in his voice. 'There are times when it makes life bloody difficult—what with Louise's social commitments and mine, we're damn lucky if we're both home more than two nights a week, and even then it doesn't always work out. . .' He broke off, his mouth twisting into the semblance of a smile. 'I'd like you to meet Louise—properly, I mean. I know you've been introduced, but I was thinking of something more social.'

Paula nodded, smiling. 'I'd like that too.'

Bill drained his coffee, staring at the empty cup thoughtfully. 'I may as well be honest; we're going through a bit of a sticky patch. Louise doesn't have many friends. . .' He shrugged. 'I think it might help if she could get to know someone—well, someone like yourself, someone she might be able to relate to, outside the bank.'

Paula shifted slightly uneasily. 'I'll be happy to meet her and it would be nice if we could be friends, of course, but. . .look, I don't want to seem to be interfering in something that may be personal, but. . .'

'Don't worry.' Bill smiled. 'It's no big secret.

When you get down to basics I suppose what it amounts to is that Louise is very happy with her work and doesn't see any reason why she should give it up to have children. Whereas I. . .' He ran a hand through his hair. 'Still, that's my problem, not yours. I just feel that Louise could do with a friend. We'll have to arrange a get-together. Here, let me get you some more coffee.'

Paula was handing him her cup when the door opened and Adam Sinclair walked in, a slightly harassed expression marring his attractive features.

'I seem to spend more time on paperwork these days, and if it's not paperwork I'm seeing sales reps.' He was wearing a suit in fine, dark fabric. His shirt was white with a dark blue stripe. Paula found herself gazing with fascination at his hair, which curled slightly against the collar, before her gaze rose and met the full impact of his amazingly blue eyes. With a start she realised he was looking straight at her.

'Sleep well?'

A small pulse began to hammer at the base of her throat. 'Like a log, thanks.' She leapt to her feet to rescue her cup from Bill. 'I'll do that, shall I? Anyone else for a refill?'

'If you're doing the honours I'll have mine black and unsweetened.'

Paula willed her hands to remain steady as she poured the coffee. Having done so, she turned, handing him the cup, and as he took it their fingers met. The memory of the few seconds she had spent in his arms came surging back, so vividly that she jerked away, spilling coffee into the saucer.

'Come to think of it,' Bill unwittingly came to her rescue, 'Louise and I are having a party in about a week's time, to celebrate our tenth wedding anniversary. Now that you've decided to stay you must come. It'll be the perfect opportunity for the two of you to meet.'

Paula sipped at the coffee she didn't really want. 'Yes, well, thanks, that would be nice. I shall look forward to it.'

'Nothing formal—a few friends. If there's someone you'd like to bring along, feel free.'

Without turning her head Paula could feel the weight of Adam's blue eyes watching her, his own expression giving nothing away as she turned slowly. She found herself wondering briefly whom he would be taking along to the party. Girlfriend? Or wife? Without being aware of it her fingers tightened round the cup.

'I haven't really had much opportunity to get to know many people yet,' she explained. 'Perhaps I can think about it and let you know?'

'Sure, that's fine. At least you'll have more time for socialising, now that you're staying.'

Paula relaxed, feeling she was somehow on safer ground. 'That's what I'm hoping.' She smiled. 'I may even get around to joining the local library. Apparently it's quite close to where I'm staying.'

'I gather you've rented a flat,' Adam said evenly.

'Mm, yes—well, flat is the agents' word. I'd say they were being a little generous. It's more like a partitioned bed-sit; fairly cramped, but it was fine for a short stay. Now that things have changed I've been thinking I may look for something a little more suitable.'

Bill looked doubtful. 'There's not an awful lot in the way of property to rent around here. What sort of thing did you have in mind?'

'Oh, I don't know—a slightly larger flat maybe, or even a house, provided it wasn't too big and I could get it on a short lease.'

'Both sound a little unlikely in Buckleigh Parva,' Adam told her. 'Aside from the local farming community, this tends to be more of a retirement area. There's not much in the way of spare property.'

'Oh.' Paula looked crestfallen, her hopes of escaping Mrs Phillips's flatlet fading fast. 'Well, I suppose if I really can't find anything I'll just have to make do. It's not exactly an ideal arrangement. I'm always conscious that I'm probably disturbing the rest of the inhabitants if I get a call out at night.' She bit her lip. 'I'll have a word with some local agents and see what they can come up with—or not, as the case may be.'

Bill snapped his fingers. 'Of course there is another possibility.' He was looking at Adam. 'How about the cottage?'

'Cottage?' Paula looked from one to the other, uncertainly.

'Sure,' Bill enthused. 'Adam just happens to have one that's going begging. How about it? You have a ready-made tenant.'

The set of Adam's mouth sugested that he wasn't at all happy with the way things were going. 'It's not quite that simple——'

'Oh, come on, you've been saying for ages that the place is falling down for lack of use.'

'That may have been a slight exaggeration. It needs some work doing on it.' There was a taut edge to Adam's voice now.

Paula felt the dull colour rising in her cheeks. He doesn't want me to have it, the thought echoed inside her head. 'Look, it's really not that important. I can probably manage perfectly well where I am. . .'

'It's not that I wouldn't be happy to let you make use of it.' His voice was curt, the message in his eyes all too obvious. 'The fact is, it hasn't been decorated for heaven knows how long, and it's bound to be damp.'

She managed to keep her own voice very cool. 'It's really not that important. In fact, the more I think about it, the more I realise it was a pretty silly idea anyway, to move out of perfectly reasonable accommodation for what is, after all, still only a brief stay.'

He was frowning, a deep cleft between the dark brows. 'Don't misunderstand me; it's not that I'm against you making use of the cottage.'

It's just that you'd rather I didn't, Paula supplied the silent dialogue.

A spasm flickered across his features, leaving them taut. 'Bill's right, it would be ideal for your needs. It's just that it isn't quite that simple.'

'Please,' she bridled defensively, 'I understand perfectly. Don't give it another thought. If I feel really desperate I can still go along to the agents, but I doubt if I shall bother.' She saw the muscle tighten in his jaw.

'I'm not dismissing the idea,' he said coolly. 'I need a little time to think about it. Give me a few days, then I'll let you know one way or the other.'

Confusion clouded her eyes as she acknowledged an inner sense of disappointment. Perhaps he just didn't like the idea of having a colleague practically living on his doorstep. Or maybe it was more personal. He didn't want *her* practically on his doorstep!

She forced a smile to her lips as she gathered up her coat and made for the door. 'Take all the time you need. As I said, there's no urgency. In the meantime, if I come up with an alternative I'll let you know.' She shot a quick glance in Bill's direction and saw a derisive smile tugging at the corners of his mouth as if he was actually enjoying the situation, though why that should be the case she couldn't imagine. 'I'll see you later, Bill—oh, and thanks for the invitation. I shall look forward to seeing Louise again.'

It wasn't until she was seated in her car that she began to relax. She was annoyed with Bill for having provoked what had proved to be a very embarrassing situation. On reflection, she thought, slamming the car noisily into gear, she wasn't at all sure she liked the idea of having Adam Sinclair for a landlord anyway. As for having him as a neighbour, it could be far too much of a distraction!

CHAPTER FOUR

PAULA aimed the latest batch of estate agents' bumf into the nearest wastepaper bin before collecting her afternoon post.

'Still not having any luck?' Gill Cleaver asked sympathetically.

'Not so that you'd notice.' Paula smiled wearily. 'I wouldn't mind, but I've explained in great detail precisely what I'm looking for and how much I can afford to pay, and they promptly deluge me with details of properties that are way above my price bracket.' She sighed heavily. 'Oh, well, perhaps Dr Sinclair will come up with the offer of the use of his cottage after all. I almost wish the idea hadn't been mentioned. I could probably have managed quite happily where I am, until I started thinking about a move.'

Gill laughed. 'I know what you mean.'

'I don't suppose you know anything about this cottage of Dr Sinclair's? Only it occurred to me that I could be building up my hopes and the place may be falling apart.'

'I can't say I do, to be honest, except that it's been empty for a while now. Such a shame, too. Not that I've been inside, you understand, but I've driven past. Come to think of it, you must have seen it. It's set back from the road, just outside of town. White with black beams, thatched roof. Parts of it date back to Tudor times, or so I've heard.'

Paula was intrigued. 'So why is such a highly desirable property left standing empty? Where I come from it's the sort of place that would fetch the earth!' And which, she thought, probably explained Adam Sinclair's reluctance to rent it out. On reflection, she decided, she couldn't honestly blame him. She wouldn't exactly relish the idea of having someone who was a virtual stranger moving in on her own personal territory. It would be like an invasion of privacy. An image of Adam Sinclair making himself comfortably at home amongst her possessions drifted into her mind, to linger disconcertingly, until she pushed it away.

'Well, I'd better get on,' she announced briskly. 'Any sign of Dr Patterson yet?'

'Oh, he won't be in till later. He's giving evidence in court today. Some local teenagers wrecked a car some months back. Bill happened to be duty police surgeon and he was called out to examine the driver.'

'Let me guess. He was over the limit.'

Gill shook her head. 'It turned out to be drugs, not alcohol. One of his mates was killed, the other's still in hospital.' She shook her head. 'Such a waste! Anyway, the case came up today and Bill has been called to give evidence.' She flicked the pages of the appointments book with a gesture of exasperation. 'It's the parents I feel sorry for.'

'I know what you mean. Sometimes it makes you wonder who the real victims are.' Paula glanced at the clock. 'Time I got started. Who's first on the list?'

'Mr Scoggins.'

'Scoggins?'

'You mean to say you haven't had the pleasure of meeting our Mr Scoggins? In that case you have a real treat in store.'

Paula tucked the bundle of case-notes under her arm, shooting her a wry look. 'Tell me the worst, without betraying any professional secrets.'

'Oh, it's no secret. It'll be about his bunions. He's been telling everyone about them for years. Oh, and he claims to be sixty-five, but he's eighty if he's a day, and, be warned, he still fancies his chances. Just keep the desk between you and him and you should be OK.'

'Be still, my beating heart!' Grinning, Paula made her way to the consulting-room, taking a few seconds to run a comb through her hair before ringing the bell to bring in Jack Scoggins.

Her cheeks were still flushed from the cold wind, adding emphasis to her green eyes. The thickness of her hair was swept back, a touch of lipstick applied to her full, soft mouth. Her gaze travelled slowly over the brightly coloured shirt and sweater and wide-belted, full skirt. Moving to sit at the desk, she rang the bell and waited. The door opened.

'Ah, Mr Scoggins. Now, what are we going to do about these bunions of yours?'

The rest of the early evening surgery passed routinely, with the usual batch of sore throats, coughs and back-aches. Paula looked up, smiling, as the last of her patients came hesitantly into the cousulting-room.

Gail Lucas, according to her case-notes, was twenty-five and looked more. Long, dark hair hung limply, obscuring one side of her face. She moved slowly, almost nervously, avoiding Paula's gaze as she was directed to the chair.

'Mrs Lucas.' Paula smiled. 'What can I do for you?'

The girl stared at her hands, seeming uncertain where to start. 'I had a bit of an accident.'

Paula waited for some further response, then, when none was forthcoming, swivelled her own chair closer to look directly at the lowered head. A livid bruise, badly covered with make-up in an obvious attempt to camouflage it, was clearly visible as the girl looked up.

Paula felt her stomach tighten. 'I take it that's how you got that?'

There was the merest nod of acknowledgement.

'Yes, I see. And would you like to tell me about this. . .accident? How and where it happened?' She wrote something on the case-notes, quickly scanning the previous record of attendances at the surgery, at the same time giving the girl a chance to consider her answer.

'Oh, it was at home—well, in the garden, actually. I just sort of twisted my foot and. . .slipped.' Gail Lucas passed her tongue over her lip, wincing as it made contact with a cut. 'I bruised my arm too, and my ribs. It's nothing much.' She looked up, her eyes wide in some sort of silent appeal. 'It'll be all right. I just need a few pain-killers so that I can get to work. Only I have to work, you see, or there's no money coming in. . .' She broke off to stare fixedly at her hands again. 'I have to work.'

Paula studied her in silence for a moment, then drew a deep breath. 'What about your husband? Does he have a job?'

'Oh, Jim. . . No, he's been out of work for a year now, ever since the factory closed down.' Gail Lucas sniffed hard. 'That's why I have to work, you see, just till he finds something else. Then I'll give my job up and we'll probably move to a bigger house. . .' Her voice broke off in something so closely akin to a sob that Paula had to resist the urge to reach out and hold the girl's trembling hands.

'Look, why don't you let me take a look at these bruises?' she urged gently.

'No! I mean, it's nothing, really.'

Reaching for a stethoscope, Paula smiled. 'Just so that I can check that you didn't do any real damage when you fell. You may need an X-ray.'

Panic again widened the girl's brown eyes. 'I'm sure I won't. Just some tablets will do.'

'I'll certainly write a prescription for something that will ease the pain.' Paula was on her feet now. 'But I really do need to check you over. Besides, I'm sure your leg must be painful.'

'My. . .my leg?'

'You did say you twisted your ankle? That's how you came to fall?'

The girl's gaze slid away. At the same time she forced a laugh. 'Yes, well, I did. Jim's always saying I'm too clumsy by half. But my ankle is fine—really, it's fine.' She was on her feet too now, looking uncertainly towards the door. 'Look, maybe this wasn't such a good idea. I shouldn't have come. I'm just wasting your time.'

'Gail, I'm here to help—it's my job. I want to help. At least let me check your ribs. If anything is broken it could cause more damage, in which case you could well end up needing to be admitted to hospital.'

'No!' Gail Lucas's head came up sharply. 'I can't do that. I've got a kid, she needs me and. . .and there's Jim. He'll be expecting me home.' She took a step back. 'Anyway, what is this? I didn't expect to be put through some third degree.'

Paula saw the stubborn set of the girl's mouth and wondered, despairingly, what she had to do to get through to her. 'I do understand,' she murmured softly. 'In any case, it may not be necessary. If your ribs are badly bruised I can give you some tablets to ease the pain and help you to sleep.' To her relief, Gail Lucas seemed to consider, then she nodded.

'OK, if you promise you'll just give me some tablets.'

'I promise. Why don't you slip off your coat and let me take a listen?'

Gail slipped off her coat and reluctantly unfastened her blouse. When she saw the darkening bruises on the exposed flesh Paula couldn't prevent a gasp of horror.

'This wasn't an accident, was it? Those bruises certainly couldn't have been caused by a fall.' Her gaze rose slowly. 'You were beaten, weren't you? Who did this to you, Gail? You must tell me.'

To her dismay Gail Lucas began to sob as she jerked away to re-button her blouse. 'No! You're wrong.' She grabbed her coat. 'I don't have to listen to this. What sort of doctor are you anyway?' She was halfway to the door when Paula called out to her.

'Gail, wait! At least take your prescription, and promise me, if ever you need help. . .'

The door closed before she could finish speaking. Paula sat at her desk, willing her breathing back to a more even level. Gail Lucas's injuries had shocked her, the more so because she knew the girl was lying. No fall could have caused such bruises, which could mean only one thing; she was lying to protect someone and Paula couldn't do a thing about it, because her patient hadn't felt able to confide in her.

It was like an admission of failure on her part, and the knowledge stung. She drew a long breath, feeling frustration begin to turn to anger. There *must* have been a way to get through to Gail Lucas. It was her job, after all.

She was scarcely aware of the tapping at the door until it opened and Adam came into the room. He wore a dark suit, the jacket unfastened to reveal a blue shirt. He certainly didn't look like a man who had had his sleep disturbed by too many emergency calls. For a moment she found herself wondering who was going to be the lucky recipient of all that charm and devastating good looks.

She rose to her feet, to replace a book on the shelf, her movements oddly disjointed. She had quite enough to occupy her thoughts without letting her imagination run away with her where Adam Sinclair was concerned. Why did it seem that he only had to be around for her natural sense of calm professionalism to fly out of the window?

Paula dragged her attention back to more relevant things. 'Can I do something for you?' she said peevishly.

His dark brows rose. 'I can always come back later.'

Her head rose and she felt the full weight of those blue eyes studying her. Warmth flooded her face and she shook her head.

'No, it's no problem.'

Now his smile, that was another matter altogether! 'I just thought you'd like to know that the police have decided not to take any action against young Steve Watts.'

'Oh?' Her interest caught, she smiled hesitantly. 'And I suppose you didn't have anything to do with influencing that decision?'

His slow smile did things to her already over-worked pulse-rate. 'In this instance my defence wasn't needed. It turned out that the bottle-throwing incident was the result of some deliberate provocation and, as several other youngsters were also apparently involved, the police can't be absolutely certain who the guilty party is.'

'So Steve Watts lives to fight another day.' She winced, realising what she had said. 'Sorry, that was an unfortunate choice of words.'

'But, alas, in the case of Steve, probably all too true. I dare say I shall hear about it soon enough, when he's in trouble again.'

'It must give you quite a lot of satisfaction, knowing that your patients have so much faith in you, feel that they can confide.' She moistened her lips, wishing there were some way to avoid his shrewd gaze.

'Paula, what's wrong?' His hands caught her arms, turning her to face him when she would have moved away. His touch sent tiny shock waves darting through her. She drew a deep breath, her face taut with strain.

'I don't know what you mean.'

His eyes narrowed. 'You're not a very good liar.

Something must have happened—you're as taut as a wound spring.'

She stiffened, trying to pull away. 'If you really want to know, I'm having second thoughts about staying on. I shouldn't have agreed. I'm even beginning to wonder if I'm cut out for this job after all.'

His face darkened. 'Were you planning simply to walk out and leave us in the lurch?' he said drily.

'No, of course not.'

His mouth twisted. 'Then don't you think you at least owe me an explanation?'

Paula sighed heavily. 'Probably.' She raked a hand impatiently through her hair. 'The truth is, I feel I've let a patient down, badly. She came to me for help and instead of giving it, of. . .of dealing with the problem she presented, I. . .' She broke off. 'I made a complete mess of it. More to the point, I may even have made things worse.' She cleared her throat awkwardly. 'There's a very good chance that when it happens again she won't dare come back to see me.'

'You're racing ahead too fast here,' he prompted softly. 'In the first place, which patient are we talking about?'

'Mrs Lucas—Gail Lucas.' She saw his expression tighten. 'You know her?'

Adam frowned. 'She moved into the area about six months ago. I seem to recall seeing her once. I sent her for X-rays. She had. . .a broken wrist, I think it was.'

Paula felt herself pale. 'Let me guess. She told you she'd had an accident?'

'Are you saying it wasn't?'

Her gaze held his for a long moment, then she sighed. 'I checked her case-notes. Since she last saw you, Gail Lucas has also seen Bill Patterson, about three months ago. The only difference was that on that occasion she had contusions on her back. Apparently she'd fallen down the stairs.' Paula's eyes mirrored her scepticism. 'I'm not at all certain that she hasn't got at least one cracked rib as a result of her latest "accident", but she wouldn't let me examine her because I made the stupid mistake of letting her know that I wasn't fooled.'

'Go on,' Adam prompted. 'I take it you made some sort of examination?'

She stared at him, her mouth suddenly dry. 'That's the trouble. Apart from the visual evidence, the surface bruising which I was able to see, I blew it. The minute I started asking questions she was out of here like a bat out of hell.' Her gaze rose to meet his. 'What sort of doctor does that make me?'

'You used your professional judgement and did what you thought best,' he said reasonably.

'I don't agree. What I should have done was to treat my patient, instead of which I was so busy trying to get at what I thought was the truth, which is that Jim Lucas is beating his wife up, that I drove her away.' Her chin lifted. 'I can't just stand by and pretend I don't know what's happening. I have to do something. *We* have to do something!'

'So what do you suggest?' he said softly. 'That we try telling him to stop? Or perhaps we could try telling her to leave him.'

'She'd never do that.' Paula drew a deep breath. 'But that doesn't absolve us from responsibility. We can't just sit back and do nothing.'

Adam was watching her, a frown drawing his dark brows together. 'Right now we don't have much choice. Besides, aren't you the person who warned against getting involved?'

Her eyes widened in disbelief. 'I can't believe you mean that!'

'I'm not saying I condone it,' he said evenly, 'but you must know that Gail Lucas isn't compellable in law. We can't force her to make a complaint, and even if we could, there's a ten-to-one chance that when it came to it she'd refuse to go through with it and take her husband to court.'

For a moment she stared at him in stunned silence. 'So you're saying it's all right for him to go on beating her up and getting away with it? But that's. . .that's worse than awful, it's barbaric! What are we supposed to do then? Let him kill her, then, when it's too late, we can persuade someone to do something?'

Suddenly his hands closed over her arms. 'You're not thinking rationally.'

Paula strained backwards, trying to push away from him. Frustratingly his grip merely tightened, sending a tingling awareness of him surging through her. She resisted it. That sort of strong-arm male tactic might work with other females, but it wasn't going to work with her. 'I'm perfectly rational,' she bit out. 'The laws protecting women in this country are archaic, you know that? But then I don't suppose you care.' She didn't know why she was raging at him, except that, for some reason, he seemed to represent everything that made her feel vulnerable. 'Any more than you probably care that your precious law is only just starting to think about making it illegal for a man to rape his wife. What sort of justice is that? I'll tell you, it's male justice, designed by men!'

'I hope you're not including me in that generalisation,' he warned softly.

Her chin rose. 'Why not? You're male.' She knew she had gone too far when his eyes narrowed to glittering blue slits.

'You have a lot to learn about personal relationships,' he ground out. 'There are far more effective ways for a man to get what he wants than having to resort to rape. But perhaps you need someone to prove it to you.'

For an instant she contemplated flight, and knew it wasn't even an option as his grip tightened, drawing her inexorably closer. Her face flamed as her body made sharp contact with his. She began to struggle as the sheer physical awareness of his body tore through her. For a moment panic widened her eyes as he lowered his head and his mouth took possession of hers with an aggressive thoroughness, forcing her resisting lips apart as his tongue savagely invaded the softness of her mouth.

She gasped at the contempt with which he took advantage of her lack of physical strength to fight him. Then, to her everlasting shame, a totally new sensation coursed through her, so exquisite, so unlike anything she had ever experienced before as her body betrayed her with its instant response. In all the times Ralph had kissed her it had never been like this.

Moaning softly, she swayed towards him. For an instant she felt him tense, then he set her free, his breathing harsh as he drew away, leaving her senses reeling in confusion. She started to protest, then became dizzyingly aware of the open door.

'Glad I caught you.' Bill's voice intruded into the tension like a thunderclap.

Only then, as the heated colour flooded into her face, was Paula aware of Adam, deliberately shielding her from the other man's gaze, giving her time to recover. She swept a hand through her hair, guessing at how she must look. She felt as if she had been savaged! Her mouth still felt swollen, her hair was wildly dishevelled where his fingers had raked through it.

'Not interrupting anything, am I?'

'Yes!'

'No!'

Their responses came simultaneously. Paula straightened her shoulders, purposely avoiding the sardonic gleam in Adam's eyes. 'Didn't you say you had some calls to make?' she rasped.

'Did I?' He raised a mocking eyebrow and she felt the colour flare into her cheeks.

'I'm sure you did. I think we'd said all there was to say, and you were right—perhaps I did over-react.'

'It seemed like a perfectly normal reaction to me,' he said softly.

Paula choked. 'That wasn't what I. . .' But he was gone, without giving her the chance to explain.

She turned to Bill, with an effort keeping her voice even. 'Sorry about that. What can I do for you?'

Bill's mouth quirked as he handed her an envelope. 'I've been instructed to give this to you in person. It's from Louise—an official invitation to the party. She's very keen for you to come.'

Paula accepted the envelope, shakily scanning the contents.

'I wouldn't miss it. I'd already made a tentative note in my diary.'

Bill frowned. 'You don't need to worry that Louise is simply looking for a friendly ear to pour her troubles into, you know.' He gave a rueful sigh. 'Sometimes I think it might be easier if she did—talk about it, I mean.'

'It wouldn't necessarily mean that she'd change her mind,' Paula warned, 'about having children, I mean. As far as Louise is concerned it isn't a problem. Some women are perfectly happy without a family.'

'I realise that. I may not entirely understand, but I think I've more or less learned to live with it. Anyway, I want you there, as a friend. Just come and enjoy the party.'

'You can count on it.' She reached for her diary, dropping it into her briefcase. 'How many guests are you expecting?'

'Oh, about thirty. It's nothing huge or too formal. Some food and drinks, a little music.'

Not a large enough crowd to lose herself in if Adam turned up.

'How's the property-hunting going?'

She gave a light laugh. 'Not very well. I'm not even really convinced it's worth bothering. No one's going to want to offer a short lease.' Especially on love! Dammit! She slammed a drawer closed in self-disgust. Since when had Adam Sinclair become a consideration in her life? She hadn't invited him into it; he had stormed in. 'I wish you hadn't said anything about the cottage,' she muttered. 'I'm sure it put Adam in a very awkward position. He may have wanted to discuss it first with his wife.'

Bill looked at her with amused eyes. 'I shouldn't think that's very likely.'

'Oh?' Paula felt her heart give an extra thud. 'It would seem the logical thing to do.'

'Logical it may be.' Bill gave a hoot of laughter. 'But then no one could ever accuse Adam and

Alison of being logical or of conforming. So why would they start now?'

A big black cloud which Paula vaguely recognised as depression seemed suddenly to be sitting just above her head. Adam was married!

Even though she had half expected it, the shock of hearing it confirmed still hit her like a physical pain. She gave a tight smile. 'It's not unusual these days for a couple to retain a certain amount of independence after they're married, especially if they both work.'

'Work? Alison? Oh, that wasn't her style at all.'

The cloud shifted slightly. 'You mean. . .'

'Alison walked out on him two years ago. They were divorced about a year later.'

Paula swallowed hard as a dizzying wave of relief swam through her. It lasted for all of thirty seconds before being lost in the realisation that nothing had really changed. Adam might be free as far as the law was concerned, but he had married Alison, presumably because he must have loved her. *She* had been the one to walk out, leaving him to pick up the pieces. It didn't seem likely he would run the risk of getting involved again—did it?

CHAPTER FIVE

WITHIN the space of a few days it seemed winter had vanished and spring arrived, and, as if to compensate for its tardiness, a late April sun streamed into the compact, modern shopping centre where tubs of brightly coloured tulips added to a general feeling of renewal.

Paula had had to fight to resist the temptation to browse. It was her first official half-day off, which meant no morning surgery. Her calls had all been to outlying farms, and she had promised herself that she would call in at the estate agents on her way back into town.

The results were as depressing as she had expected. She pushed the few papers into her bag, knowing as soon as she glanced at them that the properties were either totally unsuitable or unaffordable.

The new boutique with its colourful window display caught her eye as she walked back to her car. She hadn't actually meant to go in, just to look, and then guilt had set in. She would probably be the only person to turn up at the party tonight wearing a dress that was, even by a generous estimate, at least three years old.

'It's a perfect fit,' the sales-lady enthused, standing behind Paula to stare in the mirror. 'And that shade of green might have been invented specially for you. It's an almost perfect match for your eyes.' Her voice contained a faint note of envy which was completely lost on Paula.

She was right about the fit, at least. Turning so that she could view the back, Paula studied the line of the figure-hugging dress. She must have lost weight. A few months ago she would have needed a size twelve; now she was down to a ten, and it did look good, she had to admit. Her thick chestnut hair, free of the tidier French plait she often adopted during working hours, swept against her shoulders. Her cheeks, slightly flushed, did somehow emphasise the rare and startling green of her eyes.

It was a dream of a dress, though the price had made her wince when she looked at the label. You don't need it, the voice of her conscience pricked the bubble of enjoyment. Admittedly, the meagre contents of her wardrobe had failed miserably under careful scrutiny. The truth was, it had been a long time since she had bought something really special, for the simple reason that she hadn't gone anywhere special. What had laughingly passed for dates with Ralph had usually ended up in the nearest hamburger bar, where they had stoked up greedily on junk food to make up for meals they had missed in the dreaded hospital canteen. Not that the quality of the food had been the only deterrent. The hours they had been called upon to work as junior doctors had often meant that, at the end of a long shift, they usually went their separate ways to fall into bed, too tired to think of anything but sleep.

Paula blinked hard, realising her thoughts had drifted and that the sales assistant was still patiently waiting.

'I do like it,' she murmured, still hesitating.

'For a special occasion, is it? I'm sure you won't find anything more perfect.'

'I'm certainly tempted.' But do I *need* it? It wasn't as if there was anyone she wanted to impress, was there? She jerked convulsively back to reality, to begin fumbling with the tiny pearl buttons. 'I'll take it.'

'I'm sure madam won't be disappointed.'

'I hope you're right.'

Beaming, the sales assistant swept out, carrying the garment over her arm before madam could change her mind. She vanished, leaving Paula standing behind the curtains in her undies, the pale shell-pink bra and panties, struggling into her sensible everyday clothes.

'Madam's probably going to regret it with a vengeance when she gets her next bank statement!' she muttered though clenched teeth as she struggled to fasten a zip.

She came out of the shop into the busy precinct and on impulse headed into the nearest coffee bar, where she ate a large cream cake, drank a cup of coffee and chided herself all the way back to the surgery. This sort of behaviour would have to stop. Two impulsive actions in one day!

Mrs Cleaver greeted her with a harassed expression. 'Oh, Doctor, there's been a call for a duty police surgeon. I tried to reach Dr Sinclair, but he's unavailable, and Dr Patterson's taking an antenatal clinic.'

'That's all right—I'll take it.' Paula stopped in the act of putting her briefcase down. 'What's the problem?'

'An unexplained death. The police don't think there are any suspicious circumstances. It's Mrs Walker.'

'Walker.' Paula searched her memory. 'Oh, yes, I remember, an elderly lady, living alone. Eighty years old, suffers from arthritis.'

Gill Cleaver nodded. 'The local postman was worried after not seeing her around for a couple of days and there was milk left on the step. He decided to investigate and found the old lady lying on the floor in the kitchen. She must have been there for a while. Anyway, they need someone to check cause of death.'

'I'll go straight away.' Frowning, Paula glanced at her watch. 'I may be late getting back for afternoon surgery.'

'I'll take care of it.' Adam spoke from the doorway. He was carrying his jacket slung over one shoulder, revealing tautly muscled arms and chest beneath a blue shirt. His casually styled black hair looked as if it had been recently trimmed.

Paula had to resist an almost compulsive yet totally illogical desire to run her fingers through the shorter locks, ruffling its neatness.

She swallowed hard. 'Are you sure you don't mind?'

'It's no problem.' His gaze lingered on her own slightly windswept hair. She must look a mess, but there had been no time to do anything with it. Her look dared him to criticise.

'You look different with your hair like that,' he said evenly.

Was that different good, or different not so good?

'You should wear it down more often.'

'It wouldn't be very practical.'

'But the patients would probably love it.'

Only the patients! 'We could always take a vote on it,' she said edgily, and saw his dark eyebrows raised quizzically.

'Having a bad day?'

'Not at all.' So why was she being so snappy? It seemed Adam had this effect on her. She hauled her briefcase more firmly into her grasp. 'I probably got out of bed the wrong side.'

'I'm sure there's an answer for that.' He was looking at her with his head cocked on one side.

Was he being funny? She glared intently at the attractive planes of his face, looking for some sign of amusement at her expense. His mouth was nerve-shatteringly sensual. She drew herself up sharply. 'I have to go——'

'Wait!' His hand caught her arm, sending a mass

of ill-timed signals firing through her veins. 'Tonight.'

'Tonight?'

'The party—Bill's and Louise's party. You hadn't forgotten?'

'No, of course not.' She gave a light laugh. Chance would be a fine thing!

'In that case, I'll pick you up.'

'There's really no need. You're probably taking someone else. It's no problem. . .'

'I'm not saying it's a problem.' Blue eyes narrowed on her. 'I just thought it might solve one. It seems like a good opportunity to kill two birds with one stone.'

'Two birds?' She was beginning to sound ridiculously like an echo.

'I thought, if you're still interested in the cottage, you'll need to take a look at it. You may decide it's not suitable for your needs.' His eyes narrowed. 'Unless, of course, you've changed your mind. You've not found something else?' He seemed to have homed in on her sudden reluctance.

'What? Oh, no, it's not that.' I just don't want to get in over my head. Panic tinged the thought. There was no future in it. She looked at him awkwardly. 'It's just that. . .well, I realise you were put in a very difficult position. Bill shouldn't have said anything, and I certainly didn't expect—or want—you to take it seriously.'

'I never do anything unless I choose to,' Adam said with dry impatience. 'If I seemed reluctant, it was not because I had anything against your making use of the cottage.' He frowned. 'I simply hadn't considered the possibility of letting it.'

'I can understand that,' she acknowledged ruefully. Who would want a complete stranger stamping all over their precious memories?

'On reflection, Bill's suggestion made some kind of sense. It's been standing empty too long. But if you've changed your mind. . .'

'Oh, no—I mean, I haven't. I'd love to see it.'

'In that case, I'll pick you up after I've finished here and take you along to see the cottage,' he said evenly. 'Provided you have no objection to going back to my place afterwards, so that I can get changed before we go on to Bill's and Louise's. It seems the least complicated way of doing the thing.' He frowned. 'I'd assumed you'd want to move in fairly quickly.'

'Yes. Yes, of course,' Paula stammered. Why did she suddenly get the feeling that she was being stampeded? 'The sooner the better.'

'Good. So I'll pick you up at seven.' He strode away without a backward glance, leaving her to wonder what he would have said if she had told him it was inconvenient.

At it happened, she was ready in plenty of time. Nervousness seemed to be pumping pure adrenalin into her system!

Returning to the flat, she had called the surgery and spoken to Gill Cleaver. 'I thought you'd want to know that Mrs Walker died of natural causes,' she told her. 'I don't think the fall contributed in any way. She probably had a heart attack and didn't know a thing about it. Yes, it is, very sad, but it wasn't for want of trying on our part. She was offered the chance of sheltered accommodation and refused to take it. I don't know that I blame her for wanting to hang on to her independence.'

After ringing off, Paula made herself a cup of coffee, nibbled at a biscuit and took herself to the bathroom to indulge in a leisurely soak in her favourite foaming bath oil. Her hair, freshly shampooed, needed nothing more than blowdrying. Deliberating in front of the mirror over whether to pin it into a coil or leave it loose, she decided on the latter, brushing it until the chestnut waves shone. Her make-up she applied slightly more heavily than she would have worn during the day. The effect, when finally she slipped into the dress, was both dramatic and startling.

She was applying touches of her favourite perfume when, right on cue, the doorbell rang. Her pulse rate quickened with nervousness. Stop it! she told herself. You're behaving like a schoolgirl on her first date! Except that there was nothing even remotely childlike about her responses to Adam Sinclair.

She slipped her feet into slender-heeled sandals, then took a deep breath, nerving herself to go and answer the doorbell, purposely pausing to check the contents of her evening bag on the way.

As she moved, the fabric of the dress moved

sensuously against her hips and legs. Catching sight of herself briefly in a mirror, she caught her breath as her reflection returned a look of self-confidence which she alone knew she didn't possess.

She hesitated in the open doorway. 'Can I offer you a drink before we go?' she asked Adam. 'I'm afraid I don't keep much alcohol, but there's some brandy. . .' She broke off, aware of his penetrating gaze, raking her slowly from head to toe, lingering with disturbing intensity on the curve of her breasts, the narrowness of her waist and hips—all, she realised now, accentuated by the softness of the clinging fabric.

Panic hit her. He didn't like the dress! She stared down at it. 'Is. . .is something wrong. . .with the dress, I mean? Only Bill said it was informal.' She passed her tongue over dry lips. 'I could always go and change.'

'You look beautiful, Paula,' Adam put in softly. 'I think we'd better forget the drink.'

She glanced anxiously at her watch. 'I hadn't realised we were late.'

'We're not, *yet*,' he said tautly.

Paula swallowed hard, her breathing uneven as he ushered her towards the car, opening the passenger door and helping her in before going round to the driver's seat. It wasn't a small car, but he was still too close. She could feel the warmth of his body against hers, smell the distinctive aftershave he was wearing. Adam Sinclair was the most sexually exciting man she had ever met.

An involuntary shiver ran through her and, as if instantly aware of it, he took his eyes from the road to glance at her.

'Nervous? There's no need to be, you know. Bill and Louise have some very nice friends.'

'I'm sure they have.' She avoided his gaze, glad that he had mistaken the real reason behind that shiver. His nearness affected her in a way she hadn't dreamed possible. 'To be honest, I'm slightly nervous about the cottage too.'

Adam took his gaze from the road to look at her. 'I hope you won't be disappointed. I did warn you, it's been standing empty for months. Someone goes in regularly to keep it clean and aired, but it's not the same, is it?'

'I know what you mean. There's nothing sadder than an empty house. They need to be lived in, to be loved and cared for, pretty much like people, I suppose.' She instantly regretted the words as his eyes narrowed.

'You don't really believe people can make a house happy?'

'Yes, of course I do,' she defended stoutly.

'Atmosphere is about people,' he rasped. 'Bricks and mortar are just the shell that protects them from the prying eyes of the outside world.'

Paula was shocked by the momentary note of bitterness in his voice. It was the first time she had heard it, and there was no doubt in her mind that he was thinking of the woman who had obviously caused him such pain. She sighed heavily. How was it possible to feel jealous of someone she had never even met?

It was a relief when they drew up at the roadside and she was able to climb out of the car to gaze in delight at the black and white timbered cottage. Its thatched roof hung like wary eyebrows over tiny upper floor windows. Beyond a small gate, wild daffodils and tulips riotously displayed their colours in a garden which had obviously been lovingly tended. Her breath caught in her throat.

Adam unlocked the door and stood aside, allowing her to enter. She did so, standing in fascinated silence as her gaze swept from the large, open fireplace to darkened oak beams, the gleaming brass and chintz-covered chairs.

'It's beautiful,' she murmured.

He crossed to one of the doors. 'The kitchen is through here. Not very large, I'm afraid.' He ducked. 'And the ceilings tend to be on the low side.' He grimaced wryly as he followed her. 'The folk who built this around four hundred years ago must have been pretty small.'

It obviously hadn't occurred to him that he was also exceptionally tall. Paula gazed up at him, and wished she hadn't. A six-foot-and-then-some man, in a tiny kitchen, could be a problem in more ways than one!

She averted her eyes, taking in instead the far safer contours of a surprisingly modern kitchen with its gleaming cooker, a refrigerator and all the usual equipment to be found in most larger kitchens, except that, here, the sizes seemed to have been scaled down.

She reached up to investigate cupboards containing china and glassware. Everything, in fact, that she could possibly need, and chosen by the woman who had lived here. The thought briefly marred her pleasure.

'If there's anything you need that isn't here. . .'

'Oh, no. It's perfect as it is.'

His dark brows rose quizzically. 'You think so?'

'I don't see how anyone could help but fall in love with it.'

He looked at her for several seconds before turning abruptly to the other door. 'I expect you'd like to see upstairs.'

'Well, yes, if you don't mind?'

'You're entitled to know what you're letting yourself in for. The stairs are through here.'

She hadn't expected him to follow her, but when she reached the tiny open landing, he was behind her as she pushed open the first door.

'That's the small bedroom.'

It was a child's room, prettily furnished with a single bed, matching carpet and curtains.

'It's lovely,' she murmured evenly. Even though it did seem to have been caught in some time-warp. More like a nursery, for a small child, yet it had an untouched look about it.

'And this is the largest room.'

She felt like an intruder as she walked into it.

Again, the furnishings and curtains had been carefully chosen to create the maximum effect, an illusion of space in which the centrepiece was a large bed. She tore her eyes from it to find Adam watching her. 'I don't know what to say,' she told him.

He frowned. 'All you have to do is decide whether you're interested. If not, I've decided to put the property on the market, which is probably what I should have done a long time ago.'

'Oh, no! I mean, I love it.' She followed him downstairs. 'I'll take it, if you're sure?'

'Then I'll have my solicitor draw up the papers.'

'But we haven't even discussed rent.' She faced him. 'Surely there are things we should discuss, things you need to know?'

'You mean I should check your credentials?' he drawled mockingly.

Colour flared into her cheeks. 'Well, not exactly.'

'In that case, I'm prepared to accept whatever you think is reasonable.'

Paula stared at him incredulously. 'But that's a crazy way of doing business! Where I come from, a place like this would cost a fortune!' She chewed at her lower lip. 'Perhaps you should reconsider.'

'I never change my mind, once it's made up,' Adam said softly.

'Then at least you must name a fair price.'

'Hell,' he snapped, 'I'm not particularly interested in the local market. If I'd thought of it as a commercial venture I'd probably have sold it twelve months ago.'

Except that he probably couldn't bear to part with it, Paula thought. She searched every plane of his face. It was a wonderful journey which told her absolutely nothing, except that he had built a pretty sturdy barrier around his emotions. If only her own were as well controlled!

She moved away, using curiosity as an excuse to put some distance between them, poking her head into cupboards and alcoves, opening and closing drawers.

'I'd hate to have strangers tramping over my home,' she pronounced flatly. 'It would seem like an invasion.'

'There's nothing here that matters, and you're not a stranger.'

She turned slowly to find him watching her, an unreadable expression in his blue eyes. It could be boredom, she told herself. He must think she was behaving like a child with a new toy, but that was precisely how she felt. 'I'm surprised you let it stand empty for so long, in spite of. . .' She broke off, appalled by what she had almost said.

'In spite of?' he prompted softly.

'I. . .er. . .Bill told me about your divorce,' she muttered under her breath. 'I wasn't prying. I think he just assumed for some reason that I knew,' she finished lamely.

'It's no secret,' Adam advised her hardly. 'In a small town like this, if your wife walks out everyone knows about it, especially if you happen to be the local doctor.'

Paula stared at him. Either he was taking it very calmly or he was putting on a very good act; she couldn't decide which.

'You must have been devastated.'

He frowned. 'My emotions may have been a little confused at the time. I'm not sure I'd use the word devastated.'

She gave him a long, searching look and decided he was probably still suffering from delayed shock. For a second there was a flash of cynicism in his eyes. 'There are two sides to every coin,' he explained. 'My work took up a lot of my time. It intruded into our social life. If we went out to dinner I couldn't guarantee I wouldn't be called away on some emergency or other.'

'That doesn't sound too unreasonable to me. It's all part of being a doctor. It's hardly a nine-to-five sort of job.'

'It was part of *my* life.'

'But surely she realised that when she agreed to marry you?'

'It was never that simple.' Adam sighed. 'I hadn't been with the practice very long then. I was very young and keen.'

'It all seems like any normal, healthy commitment to me,' she snapped. Now why on earth was she getting so angry? 'I mean, it takes time to build up a practice.'

'I know that. Alison simply didn't share my

enthusiasm, I suppose. She began to resent having to leave parties early. After a while she began to stay on.' His mouth tightened. 'Finally she began staying out.'

Paula felt her anger stirring. 'But you can't blame yourself for that. What were you supposed to do? Give up your work?'

A spasm flickered across his features. 'Oh, I gave up believing it would have made any difference. Perhaps it was unfair of me to expect Alison to share the kind of life I wanted.'

An illogical flash of rebellion made her want to shake him. 'I may be wrong, but I thought marriage was all about things like sharing and give and take and. . .and roses round the door.' She glared at him. 'I suppose you're going to tell me it's all naïve rubbish. Well, I'm not sure I want my illusions shattered.'

To her surprise Adam gave a low chuckle. She felt an odd fluttering sensation begin in her stomach, as his hands reached out to gently trace the curve of her arms before he drew her towards him.

'There's absolutely nothing wrong with roses round the door.' He tilted her head back. 'I happen to be rather partial to them myself.'

'You. . .you do? I mean, you are?'

'Why not?'

Why not indeed? She sensed a tautening of his muscles, found herself gazing in rapt fascination as his face loomed closer, bringing with it the utterly sensuous mouth.

The sensation was electric. Paula hesitated only for a second, then her head went back as she let herself be swept along on a tide of emotions. Desire flared out of control, her hands reached up, drawing him closer and, with that vital, overwhelming awareness of her body's needs, another new sensation came homing in to her bemused senses. She was in love with Adam Sinclair!

For a second shock left her swaying, then she was struggling to break free. What was she doing? What was she thinking of? The fact that she was in his arms didn't mean that her feelings were reciprocated. In fact, it was all too clear that, no matter what might have happened, he was still in love with the woman he had married. Well, she wasn't about to offer herself up as some sort of consolation prize! For one thing, her pride wouldn't allow it. For another, there was no future in loving a man who could only think of her as second best. The trouble was that fighting him might be a whole lot easier than fighting her own feelings!

In desperation she drew away. 'We're going to be late,' she said breathlessly.

He looked at her, his eyes narrowed. 'Maybe you're right. It's time we left.' His voice was rough-edged as he reached for her coat and draped it around her shoulders. Brief as it was, the contact was sufficient to reawaken all the feelings she was trying so hard to suppress. 'Here, you'd better have this.'

She stared at the key he dropped into her open hand and felt her throat tighten. 'You really do want me to move in?'

'Why not?' he rasped. 'You're right, it's been empty too long. It deserves a little loving.'

It. The house. But what about his own needs? Well, she knew the answer to that. He still loved Alison.

CHAPTER SIX

PAULA felt relieved that Adam made no attempt at conversation as he drove. Her own thoughts were company enough.

Had there been any way of getting out of going to the party, she would have taken it, but there wasn't. She was committed. Her one consolation was that at least there was safety in numbers, she reminded herself, though safety from what she wasn't quite sure!

In a small nervous gesture she ran a hand through her hair. She wasn't even aware of where they were going until the car turned in through large wrought-iron gates, the headlights blazing a path on to a long gravel drive before they came to a halt.

In the darkness, which seemed to have fallen without her even noticing, she was only able to gain a vague idea of what the house must look like. It was certainly larger than the cottage, but, of the two, she was unhesitatingly certain which she preferred.

Adam switched off the engine and turned to look at her. 'I'll try not to keep you too long while I shower and get changed.'

'That's all right.' She had to drag her mind away

from a disturbingly powerful image of his tanned, naked body, slicked with droplets of water. 'Take all the time you need.' The longer the better.

Her spiky heels sank unevenly into the gravel as she climbed out of the car. His hand rested lightly on her arm.

'You'd better hold on to me. I'm afraid this drive isn't made for anything but very sturdy footwear.' His gaze had travelled to rest on her ankles and back to her face. 'I could always carry you, of course.'

'I think I can manage,' she retorted.

'Coward!' he murmured derisively.

He might be right at that! Colour darkened her cheeks as she glanced warily at the house, noting for the first time that there were lights blazing from behind closed curtains. Maybe Adam preferred coming home to a house which didn't seem dark and empty. He probably had one of those automatic timers that turned everything on and supposedly discouraged burglars. Right now she would have given anything to creep away herself, but short of volunteering to wait in the car. . . She shivered, suddenly very reluctant to be left alone with this man.

As if he was instantly aware of her reaction his arm came round her. 'It may officially be spring,' he grated, 'but this coat you're wearing is hardly sensible for these temperatures. It's damn near freezing out here. Don't you have something more suitable?'

'It's a perfectly suitable coat,' Paula muttered through clenched teeth. She could scarcely tell him that her reaction was to him and the effect he had on her, rather than to the cold.

'Well, you'd better come into the warm.' The door was open and she stepped into a large, lighted hallway. 'I'll get Annie to pour you a large brandy.'

'Annie?' Her feet seemed suddenly to have been glued to the floor.

His dark brows rose mockingly. 'Didn't I tell you? I have a very obliging housekeeper-cum-neighbour, who pops in and does various things for me.'

'How very convenient!' She couldn't resist the gibe, and she saw his eyes narrow to glittering slits.

'Not the way you appear to mean,' he said firmly. 'As a matter of fact, I particularly want you to meet her.' He turned to smile at the young woman who appeared in the doorway. 'Annie, I don't believe you've met Paula—Dr Fairley? Paula—Annie Lambert, my guardian angel, fairy godmother, all wrapped up in one neat package.'

And a very neat package at that!

'I'm so glad to meet you, Doctor.' The word 'housekeeper' took on a whole new meaning as brown eyes locked on a level with Paula's own. Annie Lambert was around thirty-five, was petite, curvy in all the right places, and she had long blonde hair. Consolation obviously came in all shapes and sizes, Paula thought uncharitably.

'Mrs Lambert.' She studiously avoided Adam's

eyes as she offered her hand to the other woman. 'How nice to meet you too.' Her gaze slid to the coat and a large bag Annie was holding, and she knew a moment's panic. 'You're not leaving?'

'As soon as we're properly organised. You know how long it takes to decide on how much to pack for one night.'

Paula's gaze shifted to Adam, whose features betrayed absolutely nothing, except a smile.

'I should by now.'

One night! Paula felt her cheeks redden as Adam's eyebrows rose quizzically. At that moment a door burst open and a red-haired child, who couldn't have been more than seven years old, rushed gleefully towards him, flinging her nightie-clad figure at his waist.

'Daddy, Daddy! You're late, and I made you some biscuits specially, only now they're cold.' One hand uncurled to thrust a greyish, lumpy object under his nose. 'I did it all by myself, and it's got currants and jam!'

Paula watched in rapt fascination as Adam took the object and gazed at it in studied admiration. 'Well, I'd say that's just about the best biscuit I've ever been given.'

'Honestly?' Blue, heavily lashed eyes, so like his own, beamed with delight, and Paula felt as if someone had reached out and tugged at her heart. Adam's daughter! Freckle-faced, so unlike him in looks, and yet, without any shadow of doubt, his.

He looked up, his gaze locking intently with hers

for a few seconds before his mouth tightened and he returned his attention to the child.

Paula swallowed convulsively, feeling tears pricking suddenly beneath her lashes. She felt like an intruder.

'Aren't you going to eat it?' asked the child.

Adam made a slight sound in his throat. 'I most certainly am! It looks so delicious I'm just not sure where to start. So much jam! And so many currants!'

Annie grinned. 'We knew they were your favourites.'

'I appreciate the thought,' he shot back at her, with an easy familiarity that did something to Paula's heart.

'Daddy, you haven't eaten your biscuit.'

'So I haven't.' Adam popped the delicacy into his mouth, chewing with apparent relish. 'There, all gone.'

'I've got lots more in the kitchen.'

His expression scarcely changed. 'I'll save them for tomorrow, poppet. Right now I have to go and get changed or I'm going to be late for Aunt Louise's party.' He looked at Annie. 'You're sure you don't mind taking Katy over to your place for the night?'

'Mind?' She ruffled the child's red hair. 'We're going to have a great time. Besides, Katy is company for my little villains.'

'You have children?' Paula's mouth was dry. Her whole system still seemed to be in a state of shock.

Annie's clear brown eyes met hers. 'Two. Jason's just nine months and Sam is five. Katy thinks Jason is the best thing since sliced bread, don't you, poppet? Just like having your own doll to play with, except that this one isn't so obliging.'

Katy studied her with earnest eyes. 'I don't like bread, Auntie Annie, but I do like Jason.' Her gaze shifted to her father. 'Only I'd rather have a kitten.' Paula became the next target. 'Do you have a cat?'

Paula glanced uncertainly at Adam. 'Er. . .no, I don't.'

'Auntie Annie does, and it just had *five* kittens,' Katy displayed the spread fingers on one hand, 'and I only want *one*.'

Paula saw Adam's mouth quiver. 'We've had this conversation before, Katy, and I've explained that it wouldn't be fair to have a kitten, not when I'm out all day.'

'But, Daddy, I could look after it.'

'And what about when you have to go to school?' He sighed heavily and looked at his watch. 'I'm going to have to get ready.' He glanced at his watch again. 'I know how you feel about the kittens. I like them too, but it's not practical. I thought you understood that.'

Katy bit at her lower lip, nodding but saying nothing. Adam bent and hugged her. 'Be a good girl for Annie. Sweet dreams, poppet.' He kissed her nose and she flung her arms round him.

Paula felt her heart melt at the scene. The two of them, so unlike in looks. She could only guess that

Katy must take after her mother, in which case Alison Sinclair must be stunningly beautiful. She swallowed hard, shivering.

In the same instant Adam straightened up. 'You're still freezing. I'm sure Annie will get you a drink while I go up and get showered and changed. I'll be as quick as I can.'

'Don't rush.' I don't want to go to this party anyway. What she really wanted was to crawl into the privacy of her own bed, in her own room, and pull the covers over her head.

She met Adam's eyes. His face was brooding. How could she ever have imagined there might be a place for her in this man's life? Because of the kind of man he was, he would never admit that he had been hurt, made vulnerable. But she could sense that the wound was still raw.

Annie Lambert had gone, taking Katy with her. Left to her own devices, Paula studied the room, her eye caught by details; the dark wood furniture, table lamps reflecting in polished surfaces, pictures.

She could hear Adam moving about upstairs, the shower running—the intimate sounds any married couple might share. Warning bells clanged in her brain. Why put herself through this anguish? she reproached herself. Think of something else.

'Pour some more drinks,' Adam called. 'I'll be down in a minute.'

Her own glass was still half full. She poured him a brandy, setting it down on the coffee table before carrying her own to sit in one of the huge, shell-shaped armchairs. She had kicked off her shoes and sat with her feet curled under her. There was something almost hypnotic about a real fire, watching the flames lick red, gold and blue around the logs.

A slight sound made her start, and she looked up to see Adam standing in the doorway. He was studying her so intently that she sat up quickly, swinging her legs down to the floor. 'I'm sorry, I didn't see you. . .' She ran a hand awkwardly through her hair. 'I forgot where I was. . .'

'Don't apologise. I was just thinking I'd rather join you than go to this damn party.' He reached for the glass of brandy. 'I suppose we'd be missed if we didn't turn up.'

'I'm afraid we might.' Her voice sounded oddly husky. He looked devastatingly attractive, the dark suit tailored to complement his strong shoulders, trousers moulded to firm thighs. His hair, still wet from the shower, was brushed back. Paula felt her breath catch in her throat. 'Besides, I have to go—I promised Bill.' Rashly she downed the remains of her drink in one gulp. 'You could probably make some excuse, an emergency call or something.'

'That wasn't quite what I had in mind.' There was an edge to his voice.

Her gaze fell. 'You have a beautiful daughter.'

'I think so.' He swirled his own brandy before draining it and setting the glass on the table.

'I suppose she inherited that gorgeous red hair from her mother?'

His expression became stony. 'Katy takes after her mother in looks. Her temperament is all mine. She knows what she wants and usually manages to get it.' Without her even being aware of it, he had moved closer, removing the empty glass from her nerveless fingers.

'Doesn't that come pretty close to sounding like arrogance?' she murmured.

He pulled her gently towards him. 'I prefer the word determination.'

I'll bet you do, she thought. She was mentally alert, on guard to evade the slightest hint of any action that might be remotely construed as threatening on his part. She was ready for him—almost.

He frowned. 'Damn, is that the phone?'

'Was it?' She relaxed. 'I didn't hear a thing.'

'No,' he murmured, and his mouth found hers.

For what seemed an eternity she stayed in his arms, feeling the steady increase of tension, the building of desire as it washed over her, threatening to drown her. Being a substitute might not be so bad. It certainly would have compensations.

The warmth of his lips was removed, letting the cold in again on her befuddled world. Her breathing was strained and uneven. She had to get away.

'Paula. . .?' Adam groaned as she stirred uneasily in his arms. It would be so easy to give in, to surrender and let it happen. He had all the advantages—strength, her own lack of will-power.

Slowly he let her go. 'I may never accept an invitation to a party ever again,' he breathed, leaving her with the feeling that she hadn't won the battle, merely postponed the war.

CHAPTER SEVEN

'I'M so glad you managed to get here.' Louise Patterson smiled her relief. A slim, petite woman of about thirty, her dark-haired, gamine good looks were dramatically emphasised by the deceptively simple, figure-hugging black dress she was wearing. She raised her voice above the music. 'I won't even attempt to introduce you formally to everyone. I'm not even certain I know all their names myself,' she confided with a wry smile. 'I certainly don't recall inviting quite so many people.'

There did seem to be rather more than the thirty or so Bill had mentioned, Paula thought, as she gratefully accepted a glass of chilled wine, guarding it as she made her way through the jostling crowd.

Adam had been waylaid the instant they had arrived. Almost involuntarily she found herself searching for him until she caught a glimpse of his dark head.

'You must help yourself to food,' Louise insisted. 'Thank heavens I over-catered! I'm afraid everyone else seems to have beaten you to it.'

'It must be nice to be so popular.'

Louise laughed. 'Most people are happy to turn out for a party, even if they're not quite sure whose. I hadn't realised before that I tend to think of people in the singular,' she admitted. 'It always comes as quite a shock when I meet them with a partner. I find it so difficult to relate to this "other half". Does that sound awful?'

'Not a bit,' Paula smiled. 'I know what you mean.' She gazed in genuine admiration at the laden buffet table. 'This looks wonderful! I missed lunch and I hadn't realised how hungry I was until now.' She caught sight of Adam, watched as he threw back his head, giving a deep-throated laugh.

'We were afraid you weren't going to make it.' Louise followed her gaze in open curiosity. 'I had no idea you and Adam were planning on coming together. I didn't realise you knew each other that well.'

'Oh, we don't. Our arriving together was more an arrangement of convenience, killing two birds with one stone.' Why on earth was she being so defensive?

Louise raised a delicately-shaped eyebrow. 'Well, whatever the reason, Bill and I will be eternally grateful.'

'Grateful?' Paula echoed.

Louise nodded, turning to study Adam, raising her hand as, almost by instinct, he looked in her direction. 'We've been trying for ages to persuade him to be more sociable. At best he's made some unconvincing excuse, at worst he settles for an outright refusal. The man has no subtlety. It's quite ridiculous, and such a waste that a man with Adam's fabulous looks should allow himself to become a virtual recluse, just because some. . .' Louise broke off, biting at her lower lip. 'Oh, dear,' she muttered uncomfortably. 'I hate gossips. I pride myself on having learned to respect a person's confidentiality. It goes with the job, you might say.'

Paula crumbled a sausage roll between her fingers. 'I know about Alison and the divorce,' she murmured. 'Adam explained. . .'

'He did?' Louise's eyes widened.

'I didn't realise the subject was taboo.'

'Oh, it's not, exactly.' Louise frowned. 'It's just that Adam isn't usually very forthcoming on the subject, especially to strangers. Well, well!' She gave a light laugh. 'And the two of you arrived together this evening quite by accident?'

Paula smiled. 'It happens to be the truth. We had some business to discuss.'

'Oh.' Louise looked crestfallen.

'I've decided to rent Adam's cottage,' Paula answered smoothly. 'You probably know I've been asked to stay on as locum for a while longer and I needed somewhere larger. In fact it was Bill who suggested the cottage. I assumed you must know.'

'He did mention it.' Louise looked confused. 'But I didn't take it too seriously. To be honest. . .' she turned to look at Paula '. . . I wouldn't have thought he could be quite so tactless, in the circumstances, knowing how much the cottage means to Adam.'

'Tactless?' Paula prompted.

'Well, yes. Oh dear!' Louise seemed genuinely

disturbed. 'The thing is, Adam's family have owned it for generations, heaven knows how far back. Adam was born and grew up there, then when he married Alison—well, it seemed perfectly natural. . . I mean, everyone assumed they would live there.'

'I'd say it's the perfect place.' Paula stared down into her glass.

Louise sighed. 'Most people would think so.'

Paula could feel the tension in her jaw. 'I can see why Alison loved it so much, why Adam is so reluctant to part with it.'

'Loved it?' Louise shot her a look of incredulity. 'But Alison hated it, hated everything about it.'

Paula felt the colour drift from her face. 'But. . . I don't understand. I assumed it had been empty for so long because. . .'

'Because it was some sort of love-nest?' Louise gave a hoot of laughter. 'Alison once referred to it, in company, as a matchbox, and a very small matchbox at that. She found it inconvenient and too small, would you believe?' Louise shook her head. 'Alison wasn't satisfied until she'd persuaded Adam to buy the house he's living in now—that huge modern monstrosity. Well, monstrosity may be an exaggeration. It's actually quite nice. Most women I know, given the choice, would have chosen the cottage, but then the only good taste Alison ever showed was in choosing Adam, and one can't fault her for that. Unfortunately she had a tendency to greediness. Her ambitions outgrew what Adam could provide.'

Paula swallowed hard on the sudden restriction in her throat. 'I had no idea.'

'No.' Louise sighed. 'I think what hit Adam hardest was not that she left him, but that she could walk away from Katy too. It's what we all find hardest to understand. As for the cottage standing empty for so long, the reason is that Adam didn't want to unsettle Katy again. She's been through so much, besides which, of course, he needs someone to look after her when he isn't there, so I suppose the house has some advantages.'

A close proximity to Annie Lambert for one! Paula took a deep breath. She was confused by a welter of emotions. What she felt for Adam was far more than sheer physical attraction, though that was certainly part of it, but what he felt in return was raw need. In spite of everything he couldn't put Alison out of his mind.

A couple homed in on them. 'Louise, it's a fabulous party! You must let me have the recipe for that salmon mousse.'

Paula's hand tightened spasmodically on her glass, her smile as transparent as the liquid it held, if anyone had looked closely enough to see.

'I seem to be monopolising you,' she apologised. 'You mustn't let me keep you from your other guests.'

'Don't worry about it,' Louise dismissed breezily. 'I've spent an hour being sociable.'

'You don't sound as if you're exactly enjoying this,' Paula prompted softly.

'Don't I?' Louise drained the contents of her glass and replaced it with another. 'To tell you the truth, it wasn't my idea to have a party. I spend my day seeing people.'

'Bill tells me you're the local branch manager.'

'Doing his usual public relations job, is he?'

'Well, I don't know about that, but he's certainly proud of you.'

A look of cynicism fleetingly crossed the other woman's face. It was gone so quickly that Paula almost managed to convince herself it hadn't existed. 'Bill has some quaintly old-fashioned notions, about a woman's place being in the home, preferably with a brood of children.'

'I take it you don't agree?' Paula trod warily.

'Oh, I have some outlandishly modern idea that there's life beyond the kitchen sink, and I happen to enjoy my work. I'm good at it. I enjoy the challenge.' Her mouth twisted. 'Let's just say that, at best, Bill and I usually agree to disagree on this issue. At worst, he finds my seeming lack of maternal instinct beyond comprehension.' She swirled the contents of her glass, and half drained it.

'Oh, I'm sure that's not true.'

'What isn't true? Dishing the dirt, girls?' Bill draped an arm loosely around his wife's shoulders, grinning as he topped up her glass with champagne. 'I think it's about time we proposed a toast.'

He waved the bottle precariously in Paula's direction. It was rescued by Adam, who seemed to appear suddenly at her side.

He stared down at her, and her pulse-rate accelerated dangerously. 'I thought you might need rescuing,' he murmured, close to her ear.

She did, though not for the reason he imagined. The air seemed charged with tension. It was coming from all directions and using her as a sounding-board.

'What shall we drink to? Ten more years?'

'Bill and Louise?' Paula suggested, floundering desperately for some kind of neutral ground.

'Happy families,' Louise threw in tautly.

Paula just happened to glance up and saw the misery register in Bill's face. Defiantly, almost, he raised his glass. 'Happy families—why not?'

It was like standing in the middle of a war zone, Paula thought faintly. A combination of brandy, wine and now champagne on an empty stomach was making her light-headed. She was aware of Adam's arm coming to drape itself loosely round her waist. It felt nice, like a shield. She could feel the tension in his muscles.

'I don't happen to believe that children are the be-all and end-all of marriage.' Louise's voice had an edge to it. 'They certainly don't hold a marriage together. Ask Adam—he should know.'

'Oh, my God!' Bill was struggling to control his own voice. A dancing couple jostled for space and Paula was suddenly aware of Adam's body pressed against hers. She felt the tautness rippling through him and found herself waiting for his anger to explode. She pitied Louise for having dared to encroach on the forbidden territory of his private grief. But his gaze was inscrutable.

Almost as if he hadn't heard, yet she knew he must have done, he looked down at Paula. 'I think we should dance, don't you?'

'Dance?'

'I think we should show willing.'

He wasn't giving her any choice. Her breathing was constricted as he drew her away from the unhappy group, taking her in his arms, moving slowly rather than attempting to dance in the modern way, apart.

'I have a feeling that wasn't very polite.' Paula looked up at him.

'Probably not. I thought it might be the lesser of two evils,' he said soberly. 'You seemed to be in grave danger of becoming embroiled in one of Bill's and Louise's little tiffs. It can be a bit like walking through a minefield.'

'I thought I was managing quite well.'

'Believe me,' he said softly, 'you'd have been out of your depth.'

But wasn't she already? The pressure of his hand on her back drew her closer, moulding her body to his.

'Is this really necessary?' she muttered sharply.

'I think so,' he drawled softly. 'We want to make it look good. Besides, having done our duty,' he glanced at his watch, 'I think we can now safely bow out.'

'Oh!' She couldn't avoid the note of disappointment that crept perversely into her voice.

He grimaced ruefully. 'I promised to cover for George after midnight.' He swept her to a halt at the spot where Louise was standing looking bad-tempered and Bill decidedly unhappy.

'We're going to bow out and leave you two to kiss and make up.' Adam's voice held teasing amusement as he leaned forward to kiss Louise.

'I'll just get your coat.'

'We'll collect it on the way out.' He patted Louise's arm. 'That way you won't need to desert your guests.'

It was all so smoothly managed that, before she knew it, Paula found herself seated in the car and the engine purred into life.

'Was it true,' she asked after a few moments, 'that you've agreed to cover for George?'

'As it happens, yes.' He shot her a sideways look that was laced with humour. 'Why? Did you imagine it was some kind of strategic withdrawal?'

'The thought did occur to me,' she admitted.

'It didn't occur to you that I might simply want to get out of there so that I could have you to myself?' he drawled softly.

Paula darted a glance at his profile. Even in the semi-darkness, she could see the tension on his features. She swallowed hard. 'I thought. . .perhaps you were angry, because of what Louise had said. I don't think she meant to be tactless. She'd had rather a lot of wine.'

'Paula, you don't have to make excuses to me for Louise. I've known her long enough to realise that she's a deeply unhappy woman. I didn't take anything she might have said personally.'

The car came to a halt and he switched off the ignition. It wasn't until she gazed out of the window at the unlit, unwelcoming darkness of her small flat that she even realised she was home.

'Even so. . .' she began uncertainly.

Adam's hand closed over her arm as he half turned to look at her. 'I don't draw any parallels between Alison and Louise,' he said in a low voice. 'There's no comparison. At least Louise is honest. Alison didn't decide she didn't want children until after we discovered she was already pregnant. She never stopped making me feel guilty. After Katy was born she vowed she'd never have any more, by which time she'd met someone else and didn't want our marriage either.'

'At least you have Katy,' Paula said softly.

'You're right,' he said simply. 'I'll always be grateful that I have Katy.'

'But. . .didn't Alison fight for her?'

He gave a harsh laugh. 'She might have tried, but I'd have fought her through every court in the land and she knew it. But Alison wasn't interested in Katy.'

Paula shivered in spite of the heat burning in her cheeks as she became aware, yet again, of the depths of emotion Adam was capable of. It would be so easy to give in to this man. His arm brushed against her, setting her heart thudding from the brief contact. Or was it the effect of too much wine? Either way, it was a dangerous combination.

'It's late,' she muttered hoarsely. 'I have to go.'

'Paula, wait.' He forestalled her attempt to open the car door as he reached across. She tried to move away, but his hands were on her shoulders. His dark, expensively tailored jacket brushed softly against her skin, sending dangerous signals to her brain. 'Don't go.' His voice was uneven as his fingers stroked the silken mane of her hair.

'Please, don't,' she protested weakly.

He leaned forward, cupping her face in his hands, urgently drawing her towards him. 'Paula, don't run away from me. Don't you know the effect you have on me?'

How could she not know? She moaned softly as his mouth covered hers, moving with frustrating sensuality. It wasn't him she wanted to run from, it was herself!

It was that last glass of champagne that was responsible for the very odd, floating sensation, she told herself as he eased her closer still, until she could feel the heat of him through the thin fabric of her dress. Her hands tensed against the solid wall of his chest beneath his jacket, and she heard him groan softly.

'Paula, I need you.' His hands raked through her hair, moved to her shoulders, followed the curve of her breasts, waist and hips, sending tremors of excitement feathering down her spine.

She moved restlessly, searching for some kind of fulfilment that seemed only just out of reach, drowning in sensations unlike any she had ever experienced before.

'You must know how much I want you,' he rasped, breathing the soft fullness of her mouth as his hands finally released the clinging fabric of her dress to claim the curve of her breast.

She gasped at the shaft of exquisite pleasure his touch sent coursing through her. This was crazy. She should put a stop to it now, while there was still time. 'No!' She dragged her mouth away from the delicious torment he was inflicting. Her senses felt drugged, she wasn't even aware of her fingers having made contact with the warm, silky smoothness of his skin beneath his shirt until she tried to draw away.

'Paula. . .'

Her head was swimming as she tried to sit up. 'Adam, don't you see? I'm not Alison.'

He relaxed his grip to look at her with narrowed eyes. 'You think I don't know that?' he asked thickly.

She shook her head, pushing weakly against him. 'I only know that I'm not prepared to act as a substitute, some sort of. . .of consolation prize,' she said bleakly. 'Right now neither of us is thinking rationally.'

She felt him tense. He stared at her, a nerve pulsing in his jaw, then, abruptly, he let her go.

'You're right. I'd hate to do something we might both regret in the cold light of day,' he rasped.

She stared at him, desolation dulling her eyes before she finally struggled upright, her fingers clutching at the open buttons of her dress as she thrust open the car door and, without looking back, walked up the steps and let herself into the flat.

It was almost a minute later before she finally heard him drive away. Only then was she able to jerk away from the door, freeing her paralysed limbs as she headed for the bedroom and flung herself, sobbing, on to the bed before falling into an exhausted sleep.

CHAPTER EIGHT

Over the course of the following few days, Paula moved her personal possessions into the cottage. The fact that George had told her to take a couple of days off made it easier. If nothing else, it had meant she avoided seeing Adam, although she was well aware that she was merely postponing the inevitable. But at least this way, when it happened, she would be more composed, better prepared.

'Take as much time as you need,' George had said generously.

'Two days will be fine. It's not as if I have a great deal to move. In fact. . .' she gave a light laugh '. . .all my worldly goods will probably pack quite nicely into a couple of cardboard boxes!'

A slight exaggeration, she had to admit, as she hauled the final box from the boot of her car, but close enough to the truth to bring home a painful awareness of just what was missing from her life. All the things she might have had, could still have, if she was prepared to live in Alison Sinclair's shadow!

Now, wandering from room to room, she eyed dispassionately her attempts to stamp her own personality into them by hanging the few pictures she possessed, by buying plants and flowers, arranging her books on the shelves. But it wasn't going to work; she knew that the moment she tried to sleep in the huge bed, only to lie awake, tossing and turning, until raw memories finally forced her to seek sanctuary in the smaller, child's room, with its single divan and Peter Rabbit prints.

Even so, she was still staring into the darkness when the phone began to ring.

Groaning with disbelief, she turned, dragging the duvet with her, to stare accusingly at the clock. *Two a.m.*! Serves you right for offering to take on the emergency calls, she told herself as she reached for her clothes and began to dress again. In a way, it was almost a relief to get into her car. At least if she wasn't going to sleep she might as well be doing something useful.

It was a road traffic accident, which, when she got to the scene, fell into an almost predictable pattern. One driver had been killed instantly; the other had over three times the legal limit of alcohol in his blood when she examined him. The ambulance raced away and, almost two hours later, she finally fell back into bed, this time so thoroughly exhausted that she was asleep almost before her head touched the pillow, only to find herself awake again at seven and sitting in the tiny kitchen, drinking her first coffee of the day. Some habits died hard.

After a morning of chores, lunch consisted of tinned soup. She was heating it through when the doorbell rang.

'Damn, now who on earth can that be?' Discarding her apron, Paula went to open the door.

'Hi.' Louise thrust a large plant into her hands. 'I thought I'd drop in to see how the house-move is going. I haven't called at a bad time, have I?'

'Oh—er—no, not at all. You'd better come in. I've got some soup boiling itself to death in the kitchen.'

Louise seemed oddly ill at ease. 'Look, I'm obviously intruding. I just wanted to see how you were settling in.'

'You're not intruding.' Paula held the door wide. 'In fact you're just the excuse I needed to stop work. You'll just have to excuse me while I rescue lunch. Come on in.' She darted towards the kitchen, switched off the gas and returned to find Louise gazing round the sitting-room.

'It's lovely, isn't it? I'd forgotten quite how nice. I haven't been here for ages—well, I suppose before Alison left.' She traced the pattern on a cushion. 'I thought it might have changed, but it's exactly as I remember it. Funny, isn't it?'

Paula felt her stomach tighten. 'I imagine Adam must want to keep it the way it was. Look, why not join me for some lunch, unless you've already eaten?'

'Well. . .'

'I can rustle up some French bread and a little cheese to go with the soup.'

'Oh, no, soup will be fine.' Louise shed her coat, following Paula hesitantly into the kitchen, where she sat at the table, toying with a spoon and making only a half-hearted attempt to eat. Finally she abandoned all pretence. 'I may as well come straight out with it—I owe you an apology.'

'Do you?' Paula managed a smile. 'I wasn't aware of it.'

Louise stirred the soup. 'I'd had too much to drink the other night. I may have said things I didn't mean to say.'

'If you did, I must have missed it. It was a good party; everyone seemed to be enoying themselves.'

Louise threw her a look. 'You're being nice. I really didn't intend launching into an attack on male chauvinism.'

'Is that what it was?'

Louise broke a piece of bread, crumbling it between her fingers. 'No, I suppose not.' She sighed heavily. 'I suppose it could more accurately be described as a defence of feminism. Not quite the same thing, is it?'

'I'm not sure.'

'You mean you've never felt the need to defend your belief in something?'

'Oh, I wouldn't say that. Being a woman and being a doctor can still have its problems, but the same is probably true of any profession.'

Louise looked at her, made a pretence at eating the soup before abandoning it altogether. 'I suppose you think I'm being very selfish in refusing to have a baby?'

'It isn't my decision. I certainly feel it's not for

me to judge. Even if you consulted me professionally, as a doctor, the decision still wouldn't be mine.' Paula hesitated. 'One thing I do know, having a baby for the wrong reasons isn't an answer. It may not solve the problem. Some women have very strong maternal feelings, others don't. Having babies isn't obligatory.'

Louise gave a harsh laugh that faded into silence. 'Do you want children?'

Paula swallowed hard. 'Some day, probably, yes. The question hasn't exactly arisen.'

'It's not that I don't want children. I just feel I want something out of life for myself first.' Louise's hands rose in a gesture of helplessness. 'I'm thirty-three. I have a responsible job which I enjoy and which, dammit, I know I'm good at. If I give it up now to start a family, by the time I can get back to it any chances will have passed me by.'

'I don't know what to say to you,' Paula murmured.

'I suppose Bill has talked to you?'

'Not really,' Paula said honestly. 'Bill and I work together. We don't make a habit of swapping confidences—besides, it isn't my job to offer opinions or advice on personal matters.'

Louise's mouth tightened. 'He's very loyal and supportive. I'm not sure. . .' She broke off, sighing. 'If only life was more straightforward!' She looked at Paula. 'I haven't discussed this with Bill yet, but. . .there's a job coming up. It. . .it would mean promotion and a pay rise, not to mention a lot more prestige. The only problem is, it would mean my moving to a larger branch.'

'Oh, I see. And you want to apply for it?'

'I'd be a fool not to.' Louise stared at her hands. 'The question is, would I be more of a fool to go for it?'

Paula drew a deep breath. Faced with the same decision, she knew there would be no competition; she would have a child. But in her own case it looked as if the question wouldn't arise. 'Is there no way you can come up with a compromise? I can't personally think of one, but. . .'

Louise shook her head, gave a brief smile and rose reluctantly to her feet. 'I shouldn't have come to you with this. It's not your problem, but I felt I had to talk to someone.'

Paula was on her feet too now. 'I've not been much help.'

'You were here—that helped. I dare say things will sort themselves out, one way or another.'

It's a nice theory, Paula thought later, even if there wasn't much evidence of it working, at least not in her own life.

Mrs Cleaver shot Paula a look of wry apology as she placed a further batch of medical cards on the desk. 'Sorry about this, but they're still coming in. It must be the tail end of the flu epidemic.'

'Or the start of a second wave.' Paula glanced at the cards. 'Is that it?'

'For this morning anyway. Those two for you—

so last-minute they made it by the skin of their teeth as I was about to close the door. Dr Patterson's still busy.' Gill Cleaver gathered the returned cards. 'I don't know why, but we always seem to get a rush when one of the doctors has a day off.'

Paula finished the letter she was writing, addressed it to a local specialist and sealed the envelope. 'Adam is due back from the conference this evening, isn't he?'

'That's right. He rang in last evening—oh, and he left a message.'

'He did?' She felt the faint colour stir in her cheeks.

'Just to say he hoped you'd settled in at the cottage and if there are any problems to make a note and he'll see to it that they're put right.'

Paula gritted her teeth, looking swiftly away. 'As it happens, everything is fine, so I won't need to trouble him.'

'Well, that's good. He sounded quite concerned. I expect he was worried because the cottage had been empty for so long.'

'I'm sure you're right.' Paula felt a quick stab of relief as the phone began to ring and the older woman headed for the door.

'Well, I'll leave you to it, then.'

Half an hour later, Paula was tidying her desk and tying up a few loose ends when the phone rang again. She reached for it, her response purely automatic, her thoughts elsewhere. 'Dr Fairley speaking.'

The voice at the other end sounded distressed and frightened. Paula was instantly alert. 'Gail? Is that you? Now. . .try to speak slowly and calmly. That's better. Now, tell me precisely what's happened.' She drew a sharp breath. 'How badly are you hurt? Yes, yes, I understand, and where is your husband now? So he's not likely to be back for a while? Good—now listen, I want you to stay where you are. Lock the doors, just in case he does decide to return, then lie down, and I'll be with you in. . .about ten minutes. No, I promise, I won't ring the police.'

Having replaced the receiver, Paula gathered her bag and hurried out to reception. 'I've just had a call from Mrs Lucas—Gail Lucas.'

Gill Cleaver's mouth tightened. 'Don't tell me, she's fallen down the stairs again, or was it tripped over the step this time?'

'I almost wish you were right. At least this time she's being honest, so it must be pretty bad. She says her husband set about her with his fists and a leather belt.'

'Oh, my. . . How is she?'

'Conscious—just, but obviously in a bad way. I'm going over there now.'

'Hadn't you ought to let Dr Patterson go?'

Paula shook her head. 'I can't do that. He's still with his patients, and we can't afford to lose any time, just in case Jim Lucas takes it into his head to go home. Besides, Gail phoned me. She may feel happier speaking to another woman.'

'But what if her husband turns up while you're there?'

'Don't worry, I won't take any chances. If he does put in an appearance I'll get some help.'

The older woman looked doubtful. 'I still think you ought to tell Dr Patterson.'

Paula was already on her way to the door. 'No time. I'll call in later.'

It took a little over ten minutes to get to the address Gail Lucas had given her. A small group of women had gathered outside and stood gazing up at the windows. Paula thrust her way past and rang the doorbell. At the third ring, just as she was beginning to panic, she saw, through the glass panel, a figure moving slowly towards the door.

'Gail? It's Paula Fairley. You spoke to me a few minutes ago. I'm alone.'

The door was opened slowly, and Paula gasped as she stepped quickly into the hallway and Gail Lucas, her face swollen and bleeding, almost fell towards her.

Paula gritted her teeth. 'Here, lean on me.'

'My arm,' the girl said dully, through distorted lips. 'I think it's broken.'

It didn't require an X-ray to tell Paula that she was right. She led the girl to a chair. 'I need to examine you, to see exactly what injuries you have.' Her stomach tightened and she felt the anger flood into her throat as she made as gentle yet thorough an examination as possible.

Finally she straightened up, dropping her stethoscope into her bag. 'You realise, don't you, that those ribs haven't had time to heal since the last time you came to see me?'

Gail gave the merest nod, her gaze flickering nervously in the direction of the door. Paula interpreted the look.

'You're afraid your husband will come back.'

'He might, and if he finds you here. . .'

'Don't worry about me, I can take care of myself.' It was said with more bravado than truth. 'You may not believe it, but most men who beat their wives are cowards at heart. Bullying and violence seem to be the only way they can deal with their own inadequacies.' She mentally steeled herself for the familiar denial, but for once it didn't come. 'I think you may have internal injuries.' She spoke softly but firmly. 'I can't take the risk that you haven't, so I'm going to have to send for the ambulance and get you admitted to hospital.'

Gail Lucas's eyes rounded in panic. 'He'll kill me!'

'He may well, if he's allowed to go on beating you.' Paula took the girl's hand, sitting beside her. 'I'm not going to question you. My priority right now is to make sure you get the medical treatment you need.' She hurried on, sensing a protest beginning to build, 'If you don't go to hospital and, as I suspect, you're bleeding internally, I can't be responsible for the consequences. Apart from the bleeding, your arm will have to be X-rayed and set, and your ribs also need X-raying and possibly strapping.'

Gail Lucas's eyes filled with tears. 'I don't know what gets into him. He loves me—he says he does.'

'Don't try to talk.' Paula swallowed hard. 'I'm going to call for an ambulance. After that, if you tell me where your clothes are, I'll pack some things into a bag.'

She made the phone call. 'The ambulance will be here in a few minutes. Just sit tight. I'll get your things and we'll soon have you feeling more comfortable.' She returned to the sitting-room minutes later with a large carrier-bag. 'I managed to find a nightie and dressing-gown, there's a comb and toothbrush. We'll see about. . .' She broke off, tensing as the door burst open and a man came into the room. It needed no introduction to tell her that this must be Jim Lucas. His unshaven face was belligerent as he looked from his wife, now sobbing openly, to Paula.

'What the hell's going on here? Who the hell are you, and what do you reckon you're doing in my house?'

Paula fought a spasm of fear as his eyes flickered speculatively over her slim frame in the neat suit and amber-coloured blouse. Even though her high heels meant that she was on a level with the man, she didn't underestimate his strength or her own vulnerability should he become violent.

She forced herself to meet his gaze. 'My name is

Fairley—*Dr* Fairley. Your wife is badly injured and needs urgent hospital treatment. . .'

'There's nothing wrong with Gail that a few days in bed won't put right. We don't need your interference. It's just a few bruises. I suppose she fell again. I'm always telling her to be more careful.' His scornful dismissal made Paula see red.

'Your wife has possible internal inuries.' Her voice sounded remarkably calm. 'If they aren't treated, as I've already explained to her, I can't be held responsible. Her arm is also broken and there's a distinct possibility that she may have several broken ribs. I wouldn't call those minor injuries, Mr Lucas.'

She saw the flicker of fear cross Jim Lucas's sullen features as he looked at his wife, and Gail Lucas's own silent terror. Paula positioned herself deliberately between the two. 'I've called for an ambulance.'

'You've *what*?'

'Jimmy, she had to do it,' Gail pleaded. 'It went too far this time, don't you see? I tried to warn you.'

'You don't know what you're talking about!' he snarled. 'You're making it sound as if it was my fault!'

Gail's eyes became stony. 'Jimmy, I can't go on pretending, making excuses for you. People aren't stupid.'

'You're saying I am?'

Paula stiffened and, as if he had become aware

of it, his tone immediately became more cajoling, less belligerent. 'Come on, love, we can talk this out, sort it between ourselves without bringing in interfering strangers.'

'I don't think this is the time for a debate, Mr Lucas. Your wife needs to rest. I don't want her over-excited.'

For an instant his eyes glittered dangerously. 'This is between me and Gail.' He turned to his wife. 'You know I love you. This is crazy—you know I don't mean to lose my temper. It just happens.'

She lifted her head to look at him with dull eyes. 'Well, it happened once too often, Jimmy.'

Even Paula was surprised by the quiet determination in her voice. 'Don't try to talk too much.'

'This needs to be said. I can't take any more.' Gail looked at her husband. 'If this is what you mean by love, I don't want it.'

'Look, we can work this out. I promise it'll never happen again.'

Gail shook her head. 'It's no good. I want to believe you, but I can't. Don't you see? It's happened too many times. I've had to make too many excuses.'

Paula stirred, her attention caught by the flashing of a blue light in the street. 'The ambulance is here.' She gasped then as Jim Lucas's hand came down on her arm, tightening in a steely grip.

'You put her up to this. She wouldn't have done it if you hadn't interfered.'

She tried to free herself, a knot of fear tightening in her stomach. She found herself wishing, desperately, that Adam were here. He would know what to do. But he wasn't. Knights in shining armour only existed in books. 'Let me go, Mr Lucas, you're hurting me!'

'That's nothing,' he sneered. 'You're good at dishing out the medicine. How would you like to take it for a change?'

She flinched as his hand rose, heard Gail call out, 'Jimmy, no! It won't do any good, not this time.'

The door was flung open, a voice broke in on the scene, then a uniformed figure appeared in the doorway, closely shadowed by another. Reg Watkins took one look at Paula's white face and read the situation.

'Need a hand, Dr Fairley? I understand you've got a patient for us?'

She felt her arm released and stood, swallowing hard, feeling the bruise begin to throb. 'Reg! Yes, it's Mrs Lucas. Be careful; I think there may be internal injuries.'

'You leave it to Mick and me, Doctor. We'll soon have the little lady nice and comfortable.' He broke off as Jim Lucas made a rush for the door, swearing as he went. 'Are you all right, Doc?'

Paula smiled faintly. 'I think you arrived in the nick of time, Reg. It could have turned out to be two patients instead of one!'

'They don't call us the cavalry for nothing. Now,

love. . .' he smiled at Gail, '. . .you just relax and leave all the work to us. Mick here's a good strong lad. Ever been in an ambulance before? No? Well, we'll give you the extra-special guided tour, then, complete with commentary.'

Gail smiled wanly at Paula from the stretcher. 'Thanks for everything. I should have listened to you in the first place. If. . .if it's any consolation, I've decided to press charges this time. Jimmy needs saving from himself. He's really a good man. He doesn't mean to do what he does. . .'

'Just rest,' Paula said softly. 'Talk later.'

'OK, little lady?' Reg glanced at Paula. 'We'll be off, then. See you later, Doc.'

Paula nodded. Suddenly she felt exhausted; her arm ached where Jim Lucas had grabbed at it. There was sure to be a bruise later. Altogether it had been a mixed sort of a day, so far.

CHAPTER NINE

SHE had been right about the bruise. Ruefully, Paula surveyed the darkening area above her elbow as she gazed in the bathroom mirror. A long soak in a warm bath had helped to ease some of the tension in her muscles, and in spite of the fact that it was early evening she slipped into a nightie and a silk robe and decided to put up her feet and relax.

In fact it was easier said than done. Even the tiny element of triumph she might have felt at Gail Lucas's decision to press charges against her husband was negated when she remembered the moment of fear she had felt when confronted by Jim Lucas.

Never before had she been made so starkly aware of her vulnerability. For those few seconds, as her brain refused to function, her one thought had been of Adam. In fact, she decided restlessly, he was becoming altogether too much a part of her thinking lately, and she found the realisation deeply disturbing. How could the feeling have grown in so short a time?

She tried telling herself that she respected his professionalism. It was true, but her feelings went far deeper than the respect of one colleague for another, a colleague she could happily leave behind, but when the time came, as it shortly must, to leave Buckleigh Parva, it would be like leaving a part of herself, and she wasn't at all sure how she would cope with a life in which Adam didn't play a part.

Curled up in a chair, Paula closed her eyes. Her favourite classical music, playing softly on the stereo, filled the background but did nothing to drive away a feeling of depression. The more she thought about it, the more ludicrous it seemed that here she was, an intelligent, fully grown woman, who spent her days handing out pills and panaceas, sorting out other problems, yet she was incapable of solving her own. Half a loaf is better than none, her mother had always used to say, but loving Adam and receiving only half a love in return could only result in even more heartache.

It must have been the music, combined with the hypnotic effect of the fire, that made her drift into an exhausted sleep. Whatever the cause, her dreams were no less troublesome.

It was the insistent ringing of a bell which finally roused her, until she shifted restlessly, returning to wakefulness as she realised that the sound was actually coming from the front door.

Dazed with tiredness, she moved stiffly to open it, and stared at the figure standing there. Her pulse quickened as concern overcame surprise. 'Katy! What are you doing here? I wasn't expecting visitors.' She opened the door wide. 'Have you come alone?' She peered above the little red-head into the semi-darkness and felt her sense of alarm increase.

'I came to see you.' The small, jeans-clad figure gazed up at Paula. 'You're not going to bed, are you? *I* don't go to bed till half-past eight, and I'm only seven.'

'You'd better come inside.' Paula ushered Adam's daughter into the sitting-room. 'No, I'm not going to bed. I just had a bath and. . . Katy, does your daddy, or anyone, know you're here?'

One lip jutted rebelliously forward. 'No.'

Paula ran a shaky hand through her hair. 'Well, look, I really think we ought to let him know. He'll be awfully worried if he doesn't know where you are.'

Uncertainty briefly clouded Katy's eyes, then she shrugged. 'I 'spect he'll only be cross, like he was when I took one of Annie's kittens home. It was only this big.' She cupped her hands. 'It could have slept in my bed with me, but Daddy said no and he made me take it back.' A tear welled up. 'It didn't want to go. It licked me, on my hand, here.' She held out a grubby hand, and Paula smiled weakly.

'Oh, dear! But I'm sure Daddy didn't mean to be cross. It's just that kittens need their mummies until they can drink milk from a saucer.'

'But I could have showed it how.'

Paula sighed heavily. 'I tell you what, how would *you* like some milk and. . .and a chocolate biscuit?'

'*Two* biscuits? I'm seven. I always eat two biscuits.'

'Then two it shall be. Why don't you sit here and watch television while I go and fetch them, then perhaps we can have a chat and you can be my visitor.'

Paula escaped to the kitchen, picked up the phone and dialled a number. It was answered almost immediately, as if the person at the other end had been sitting by the phone.

'Yes?'

'Adam, it's Paula.'

'I know who it is.' His voice sounded rough-edged with tension.

'I thought you ought to know that Katy is here.' She heard his sharp intake of breath.

'She came to you?'

'Yes. Apparently she came visiting. I think she's a little upset. Something about a kitten?'

There was a moment's silence. 'I've been half out of my mind with worry. I was just about to call the police.'

'Well, there's no need; she's sitting in front of the TV, about to enjoy some milk and biscuits. I promise you, she's perfectly all right and making herself at home.' There was no immediate answer and for a moment she wondered whether he had heard. 'Adam?'

'I'm here,' he breathed. 'I'm sorry, I'll be over.' The receiver went down, and Paula returned to the sitting-room with a glass of milk and a plate of biscuits.

'I spoke to Daddy. He's on his way to fetch you. He was very worried.'

'I suppose that means he'll be cross again.'

Paula smiled. 'I'm sure he'll be more relieved to know that you're safe. Leaving home without telling a grown-up where you're going isn't a very good idea.'

Katy considered her seriously, then a smile broke through. 'Why don't you have one of Auntie Annie's kittens? Then I could look after it for you.'

Paula made a slight choking sound, then sighed with relief as a car drew up and, seconds later, the front doorbell rang.

Adam stood there. He was wearing dark trousers and a black sweatshirt. He looked tired.

'I'm sorry about this.' Lines of strain and tension were etched round his mouth and eyes.

'It's no problem.' Paula stood back, letting him in. 'As a matter of fact, I've enjoyed having Katy here. We had a nice chat and she's ensconced in front of the TV drinking her milk and eating biscuits.'

Adam frowned. 'I don't want her to get the idea that this is some sort of bolt-hole, or a second home,' he said tersely. He followed as she led him through to the kitchen to switch off the pot of coffee she had put on to brew. She did so, turning to face him. His glance brushed over the silk robe she was wearing, and suddenly she was aware of how thin it was, and how little she had on beneath it.

She felt the colour rise faintly in her cheeks. 'I

think you're worrying unnecessarily. There's no earthly reason for Katy to think of this as a second home.'

His mouth tightened. 'It hadn't occurred to me that she would think of it—or you—at all. It seems I was wrong, on both counts.'

She forced a light laugh. 'I don't think I figured much in the scheme of things.'

He stared at her, his dark eyes narrowed. 'That you figured at all is something I wasn't prepared for.'

She ran a shaky hand through her hair before turning away to pour coffee—anything to keep herself occupied. 'I gather Katy was upset.'

'That damn kitten again!'

She handed him a mug of coffee. 'It seems to mean a lot to her.'

A smile tugged at his mouth. 'So she came to you for sympathy, or was it moral support? Why do I get the feeling I'm outnumbered here?'

'Oh, but you're not. I mean. . .the only reason Katy came to me. . .'

'Was because you're here,' he murmured thoughtfully, before letting his glance leave her face to brush over the small changes she had made in the kitchen. 'I see you made yourself at home.'

With a touch of apprehension she followed his gaze, taking in the few colourful dried flower arrangements, the glass storage jars, a small microwave oven. 'I hope you don't mind.'

'Mind?' His dark brows drew together. 'The

cottage is yours, to do as you like with. Did you make those?' He indicated the flowers.

Paula nodded. 'Not exactly professional, maybe, but I enjoy doing them, and they add a homely touch.'

He didn't answer straight away. They stood facing each other like adversaries, yet the tension sparking between them had nothing to do with anger. Far from it; it was something far more subtle, more dangerous.

Paula's gaze was drawn to the firm line of his jaw, the sensuous mouth and dark eyes which seemed to be having a strangely hypnotic effect, drawing her towards him.

'Paula. . .'

'Adam, I. . .' she started to say, then the kitchen door burst open.

'I finished my biscuits—Daddy!' Katy eyed her father warily. 'I was just visiting.'

Adam's gaze hardened. It was as if a shutter had slammed down again, Paula thought.

'Don't you realise how worried everyone has been?' he asked solemnly. 'I've explained to you that you must never go away from the house without telling someone first.'

'But you were cross.'

Adam's jaw tightened as he knelt and ruffled her hair. 'I just wish you could understand. I know how much you want a kitten, but kittens need lots of love and attention, and kittens grow up.'

'I know.' The smaller jaw trembled slightly.

Adam sighed as he straightened up, one hand resting on his daughter's shoulder. He looked at Paula and gave a wry smile. 'This is one stubborn young lady. It looks as if I'm going to have to learn to live with being the villain of the piece.'

'It does rather, doesn't it?' Paula offered crocodile sympathy. 'Er. . .and who did you say she takes after?'

A nerve twitched in his jaw. 'That was definitely below the belt, Dr Fairley.'

Her chin rose. 'Oh, I'd say it was just about on target, Dr Sinclair.' She smiled sweetly, aware of the child, gazing up at them, a frown disfiguring her small face.

'Are you talking about me?'

Paula bit at her lower lip as she shot Adam a glance, then she bent and kissed Katy on the cheek. 'Not really, poppet. It was just a sort of grown-up joke, and not a very good one at that.' She became aware of Adam watching, and wished she knew what he was thinking.

'I suppose you'll be leaving too?' Katy queried guilelessly.

Paula heard Adam draw in a breath and suddenly found herself having to battle to keep her own breathing even. 'I'm not sure what you mean.'

The blue eyes that met hers held a challenge. 'Mummy went away. I 'spect it was because I was naughty.'

'Oh, Katy, no, I'm sure that's not the reason.' Paula flung a look in Adam's direction, and this time there was no mistaking the strain on his face. 'People don't leave just because someone is naughty,' she floundered helplessly, realising she was getting on to dangerous ground. How much did the child know about what had happened? She knelt quickly to take Katy's small hands in hers. 'If. . .when I leave here, it won't be because of anything you've done, it will simply be because my work here is finished. Can you understand that?'

'Of course,' came the scornful reply. 'I'm seven, not a baby. But I'd like you to stay. Daddy would like you to stay.'

Paula straightened up, feeling the tide of colour wash into her cheeks. 'I'm afraid it isn't quite that simple.' She sighed heavily. In fact, nothing was simple any more. Her whole life seemed to have become complicated from the moment Adam Sinclair had walked into it, and it was getting worse by the minute. What was more, it was unfair. As if she were walking on quicksand—the more she struggled to break free, it seemed the deeper she was being sucked in.

She closed her eyes and opened them again to find Adam watching her, his expression, as before, shuttered, unreadable. No help there.

She tightened the belt on her robe. 'I'm sorry—I'm tired. It's been a long day.' The bruise on her arm ached, but not nearly as much as her heart. 'If you don't mind. . .'

Adam's hand closed over Katy's shoulder. 'I'll try to make sure you're not disturbed again.'

Easy to say, she thought as she closed the door behind them, listening for the car to drive away. The trouble was, where Adam Sinclair was concerned, out of sight was definitely not out of mind!

CHAPTER TEN

SPRING arrived with a vengeance in the week that followed. Suddenly the trees were in full bloom and, with the passing of the flu epidemic, life, on the professional front at least, became easier.

Where Adam was concerned, careful avoidance became the order of Paula's day, and it seemed he was adopting the same principle, because she hadn't seen any sign of him for several days. Perversely, she found herself looking for his car as she drove into the small car park after seeing the empty space three days in a row.

Perhaps he'd taken it into the garage to be serviced. Perhaps he had gone away for a few days. All to the good, she lectured herself firmly. What he does with his private life is no concern of yours.

Paula did a hasty recount of her patients' cards as a tap came at the door, just as she imagined she had seen out the last of the afternoon's patients.

[illegible]

doorway. 'Hi. Look, if this is a bad time. . . I know I should have made an appointment.'

Paula was instantly on her feet. 'No, of course it's not inconvenient. I'm glad to see you. You took me by surprise, that's all. I thought I must have missed a patient or something.' Smiling, she gestured towards the chair. 'Take a seat. Do I take it this is not entirely a social visit?'

'Actually, no.' Louise bit her lower lip. 'I came on the offchance that you'd be able to see me, but if it's awkward. . .'

'No, of course it isn't.' Paula frowned. 'But are you sure you wouldn't rather see Bill, or George?'

'Heavens, no! That's the last thing.' Louise sighed and unbuttoned her coat. 'I took the day off from the bank. Bill doesn't even know.' She glanced up, and Paula noted the pallor in her cheeks. 'Well, there was no reason to tell him, really. I probably shouldn't be wasting your time.'

'You're not.' Paula was quick to offer the smiling assurance. 'Stop worrying about it. For once I don't have any calls, and I'm due for a coffee break. Would you like some?'

'No, thanks.' Louise shuddered. Her gaze met Paula's and fell away again. 'To tell you the truth, I've been feeling a bit off colour for a while.'

'Can you say how long exactly?'

'I can't be certain. I wasn't feeling too good the last time I saw you, at the cottage.'

'Why on earth didn't you say something?'

Louise shrugged, brushing a hand through her hair. 'Oh, I don't know. It's nothing specific. That's the trouble, I'm beginning to think it's all in the mind—you know, psychological, to cover a guilt complex.' She sighed. 'I suppose I noticed it shortly after the party. A couple of days, a week, maybe.' Her mouth formed a wry grin. 'It's probably indigestion.'

'If it is then it's a little prolonged.' Paula smiled easily. 'Either way, it's obviously troubling you enough to bring you here, so let's see if we can sort things out. Suppose, to begin with, you try and tell me what sort of symptoms you're getting.'

'But that's the trouble—it's all a bit vague.' Louise made a dismissive gesture with her hand. 'Headache, dizziness, weepiness.'

'Off your food.'

There was a moment's hesitation. 'Mmm.'

'A feeling of constantly needing to spend a penny?'

Louise laughed. 'You could say! I do seem to have had a bit of a chill in my bladder lately.'

Paula sat back in her chair. 'You're sure you've only noticed the symptoms fairly recently?'

Louise frowned. 'Well, now that you mention it, no, I'm not absolutely certain. I've been so busy at work, and with the possibility of the promotion in the offing and wondering how Bill would take it—oh,' she sighed, 'you know how it is. It's hardly surprising that I get the odd dose of heartburn.'

'But is it just that?' Paula leaned forward. 'Is it indigestion, heartburn or nausea?'

Louise stared at her in silence for a moment. 'All three.'

'Ah!' Paula toyed with a pencil on the desk. 'Do you mind if I ask you something? This is personal interest rather than professional. Were you getting the symptoms when you came to see me at the cottage? When you first mentioned the possibility that you might be in line for promotion?'

There was another, slightly longer silence. 'I suppose I was.'

Paula nodded, dropped the pencil on to her desk and stood up. 'Look, to begin with, I'd like to give you a general check-up. Did you think to bring a urine specimen?'

Louise produced a small bottle from her bag. Hesitantly she handed it over as she rose to her feet. 'Do you have any idea what the problem might be?'

Paula raised an eyebrow. 'Don't you?'

'I'm pregnant, aren't I?'

'I'd say it seems highly likely. It's probably too early for me to be able to tell from an examination, but we can do a test. I can probably let you have the results in twenty-four hours. Now, how about starting with your blood-pressure?'

Ten minutes later, examination completed, she studied Louise. 'Well, I'm as sure as I can be that you're in the early stages of pregnancy. So. . .' she poured a cup of coffee, handing it over before carrying her own to the seat beside the desk '. . .the question is, how do you feel about it?'

Louise stirred her coffee but made no attempt to drink it. 'It's going to take a bit of getting used to, even though I'd begun to suspect.'

'I take it it was an accident?'

Louise gave a short laugh. 'I forgot to take my

pill. We'd been to a party, and Bill and I were both a little the worse for wear. I just didn't think—well, I hoped. . .I mean, once. . .'

'That's all it takes.'

Louise nodded, staring into her cup. 'Actually, now that it's all settled, so to speak, I quite like the idea of having a baby. As long as it wasn't on the list of probabilities I told myself it was a decision I could postpone for as long as I liked. There was time for that sort of thing later.'

'After the promotion?' Paula said evenly.

Louise looked up with a ghost of a smile. 'To be honest, I don't think I stood much of a chance. There's a lot of competition, and I'm not the most experienced candidate.' She shrugged. 'I suppose I just fancied the idea.'

'I imagine Bill is going to be highly delighted about the baby.'

Louise's face clouded. 'I'd rather he didn't know, not for a few days anyway. I. . .I need time to adjust properly to the idea myself. I'm not sure I'm ready to be smothered, or treated like a mother-to-be, just yet. I'm still myself. I still have a job to do.' Her voice trailed off. 'I'd like official confirmation of the test first.'

'That's perfectly understandable.' The distant ringing of a phone sounded in one of the other consulting-rooms. It stopped with a suddenness that surprised Paula, since she had imagined that the other surgeries had finished by now. 'You know that anything between doctor and patient will be treated as completely confidential.' She smiled as Louise rose to her feet. 'That goes for friends too. I'll ring you as soon as I get that result.'

'At the bank, not at home.'

'At the bank,' Paula confirmed smilingly as she walked to the door. She was standing in the corridor, watching Louise walk away, and was musing gently to herself on the way someone's life could be so utterly changed in so short a space of time, when the door of the room opposite burst open and Adam was standing there. He looked tired. Worse than tired, she was shocked to see, he looked haggard, or was it just that she hadn't seen him for a few days? An indefinable sense of longing swamped her.

'Adam! I didn't know you were in.'

'I'm not, officially. I decided to take a few days off. I called in to collect a few books. It's just as well I did,' he said grimly. 'That was George's wife on the phone.'

'Margaret?'

'I need you to come with me. There's been an accident. She's fallen from her wheelchair.'

'Oh, no! Is she hurt?'

'She says she's OK, but she's alone. George is at some damn meeting and she can't get up.'

'I'll be with you in a few seconds—let me just grab my bag. We can take my car.'

Mercifully it was a short drive to George Reynolds's house. When they got there, Adam didn't waste time trying the front door, but headed straight for the rear, letting them both in.

'She managed to reach the phone, so she'll be in the sitting-room.'

Paula followed blindly. At one point she stumbled over something. Adam's hand shot out to steady her, and she couldn't help wincing as his fingers made contact with the darkening bruise on her arm. He released her instantly, but not before she had seen his mouth tighten.

'Margaret!' His strode swiftly in the direction of the faint, answering call.

'Through here.'

Paula gasped as she saw the figure lying sprawled helplessly on the floor. Margaret Reynolds managed to smile as they reached her.

'I'm so sorry about this. I feel so stupid. Such a silly thing to have happened!'

Adam was a man of speedy reflexes. The reassuring smile was an added bonus. In one calm, unhurried movement he was kneeling beside her to begin a gentle examination. 'I don't want to move you until I'm sure nothing's broken,' he said. 'Better be safe than sorry.'

'I'm all right, really.' Margaret Reynolds waved a vague hand as Paula reached for a pillow to place under her head. 'I feel so silly, so very foolish.'

'What happened exactly?' Paula asked.

'That's the trouble—it was entirely my own fault. I was trying to reach my book. I dropped it, you see.' Tears glistened faintly behind the older woman's lashes. 'I'm just not used to being stuck in my chair. I. . .I forgot.'

'Don't worry about it,' Adam said gently, his expression relaxing as he straightened up. 'At least nothing's broken. You may have a couple of nasty bruises that will make their presence felt for a few days, but, apart from that, you're lucky. I'm going to lift you back into your chair. Leave it entirely to me; you're only a feather-weight.'

'I'll make you a cup of tea.' Paula headed for the kitchen. 'Don't worry, I'll find everything.' She returned minutes later with a tray to find Adam, sitting on the sofa, holding Margaret's hand. They were both laughing and Paula was pleased to see that all trace of tears had gone.

'We'll have to get some sort of alarm system,' he was saying gently. 'You know it makes sense—either that or George will have to arrange for someone to be here when he has to go out.'

'I'll settle for the alarm,' came the unequivocal response. 'I'm not ready for a baby-sitter, not yet anyway.'

'It may not come to that. You could have a remission. In the meantime, the trick is in learning to adapt, as well as possibly adapting things around the house to suit you.'

'How are you feeling now?' Paula asked, moving to sit beside her.

'A little shaken, very foolish, otherwise fine.' Margaret glanced anxiously towards the window at the sound of a car on the drive. 'That will be George. Oh, dear, I wish he didn't have to know. He has enough to think about without the added worry of wondering whether I can be left alone.'

'I'm afraid it's too late. He'll already have seen my car,' Paula murmured.

'There's no reason why this can't have been a social visit,' Adam intervened. 'I'm not saying we should hide the truth about your accident, but I see no need to dramatise it, do you?'

It was only later, after she found herself being ushered into the car, that Paula realised she had been relieved of her car keys and was sitting in the passenger-seat while Adam drove. It also occurred to her that she was happy to let him take charge.

Closing her eyes, she shivered as a build-up of tiredness and reaction set in. Louise had clung stubbornly to her independence for so long, only to relinquish it willingly in the end. While for Margaret Reynolds there was no such choice. It was a very levelling thought and, without being aware of it, Paula sighed.

'Penny for them.' Adam's voice, coming out of the semi-darkness, brought her back to reality.

'I was wondering whether I'd have the courage to cope with something like that,' she admitted bluntly.

He half turned to glance in her direction. 'People seem to find the courage from somewhere.'

But then Margaret had George. It was ludicrous that she should suddenly envy Margaret Reynolds, of all people.

The car drew to a halt and she sat gazing out of the window, only then noticing that they were at Adam's house, not the cottage. But of course, she realised, it made sense, since he had left his own car behind at the surgery.

She stirred reluctantly. Suddenly the prospect of going back to the empty cottage, alone, seemed less than inviting.

'Come in for a drink. I don't know about you,' he muttered, 'but I need one, and I hate drinking alone.'

Put like that, how could she refuse? Besides, she thought, as he put the key in the lock and stood back to let her walk into the house, Katy would be home with the redoubtable Annie.

In fact the house seemed strangely quiet.

'She's gone to stay with my parents for a few days.' Adam spoke in answer to her query. 'I must have forgotten to mention it.' He poured one large brandy and a smaller one, topped up with soda, which he handed to her. 'It gives me a chance to get some work done in peace.'

So why, Paula wondered, did she get the impression that he missed his daughter? Could it be because his desk looked remarkably uncluttered for someone who pleaded pressure of work? Or that he picked a ragged-eared teddy bear from the chair and stood gazing at it, a tiny frown etched between the dark brows before he finally set it down again.

'You miss Katy, don't you?'

'She needs other company,' he replied slowly. 'My parents dote on her and she on them. It won't do any harm for her to be spoiled rotten for a few days.'

'She's a very lucky little girl, having so many people to love her,' Paula said sincerely.

'Everyone except the one person who matters.' Adam set his glass down with a look of distaste, as if the taste of brandy had suddenly turned sour.

Paula took a deep breath, setting her own glass down. 'Aren't you being a little unfair to yourself? Katy is a perfectly well adjusted, happy little girl.'

'I'd like to believe it. Right now she's only seven.'

'And in your mind you already have her growing up a delinquent?' Paula scorned the idea. 'Why don't you start giving yourself a little credit? You've done a good job so far.'

'You're an expert, are you?'

Paula felt the colour coming to her cheeks. 'I don't claim to be that,' she retorted hotly, 'but I do remember what it was like to be Katy's age.'

'All those years ago?' he said softly. 'Is it possible?'

She realised then that he was laughing at her. 'I'm being serious.'

'So am I.' His blue eyes looked frowningly down into hers. 'I realise there are things I can't do for Katy. Things only a woman can do.'

'Children are amazingly resilient and resourceful.'

'Do you have an answer for everything?'

'I try,' she snapped, finding his nearness illogically unnerving. Why did everything about this man have to be so. . .likeable? No, more than that, so infinitely desirable?

She sighed without being aware she had done so. Instantly his hands were on her arms. She flinched again, this time rubbing at the bruise. Adam was on to it in a flash, pushing her shirt-sleeve aside, his mouth tightening, then, oddly, relaxing as he stared at the darkening area.

'When did this happen?' he asked, in a quietly controlled voice.

She tried in vain to draw her arm away. 'A few days ago.'

'Who did it?'

He really didn't have to make an issue of it. She was perfectly capable of looking after herself. 'It's nothing. A slight encounter with Jim Lucas.'

'I see.' Before she knew what he was doing, he bent his head, brushing his lips over the bruise, but not stopping there.

Even as she stood, caught completely unawares by the gesture, his expression changed. He trained in with deadly accuracy on a new target—her mouth. The effect was as devastating as it was confusing. Resistance was a word that seemed to have been wiped from her vocabulary. That wasn't to say there wasn't a little hesitancy, but, when two immovable objects suddenly collided, something had to give.

Adam raised his head long enough to look at her, a question in his glittering blue eyes. She answered it breathlessly by raising her face to his. 'This is crazy,' he breathed harshly, before his mouth descended again.

She had to agree, it was utterly crazy. But she would think about that later—much later.

CHAPTER ELEVEN

GEORGE closed the door, tapped the stem of his empty pipe on the palm of his other hand and came directly to the point.

'I'd like to thank you both for what you did for Margaret. I know, I know. . .' he held up his hand, cutting short a joint protest '. . .as it happens she wasn't hurt, but if you hadn't gone out, as you did, in answer to her call—well, God knows how long she might have been lying there.'

'George, it was nothing,' Paula insisted. 'I'm only glad Margaret wasn't injured.'

'And I'm just thankful we happened to be here.' Adam eased himself upright from where he had been half sitting, half standing against the desk.

'Either way, I want you both to know that I'm grateful. I'd never have forgiven myself if anything had happened.' George sucked at the still unlit pipe, frowning as he ran a hand through his greying hair. 'The truth is, it's made me do some serious thinking about problems I knew would have to be faced sooner or later. I just kept telling myself they would be later. Well, it seems I was wrong.' The pipe wavered. 'I've decided it's time to retire.'

Paula's throat tightened painfully. She was aware of Adam tensing as he moved towards the desk.

'Don't you think you might be over-reacting?' he said quietly. 'I see what's behind your reasoning, George, but nothing happened beyond the fact that Margaret was shaken up, a little frightened.'

'But don't you see, that's just the point. She wouldn't have been if I'd been there. It wouldn't have happened.'

'You can't be with her twenty-four hours a day.' Paula frowned. 'With the best will in the world, would either of you want that?'

George smiled at them both. 'No, of course not, and that's not what I'm suggesting. But I now know I've been rather selfish. I'm sixty-three, and Margaret's nearly sixty. I've always had my work. Margaret gave up a good job herself when this damned MS took a hold. What I hadn't realised was that she didn't just give up a job; she gave up her friends, her colleagues, the stimulation of doing something worthwhile, and there hasn't been anyone or anything to fill the gaps. Most of all, it comes down to me.' He sat back, looking at them. 'I thought I was doing the best thing, working my time out.' He shook his head.

'The practice needs you, George.'

'I could carry on here for another year, two years, five, maybe. We certainly wouldn't have any financial worries. But I'd also be nearer seventy by the time I eventually did go. Margaret. . .may not be as well as she is now, and nothing we could do would bring the years back. So I came to a decision. I realise it's rather sudden. I understand it's bound to cause a few problems, but I've decided to spend as much time as possible with Margaret. I thought a cruise to start with, somewhere warm. I'll have a chat with her about selling the house and buying a bungalow, and next winter we could fly off to Spain and enjoy some sun.'

Paula looked at Adam. She watched the varying emotions flickering over his face and knew he was shocked.

'You certainly seem to have thought things out.' He dug his hands into his pockets. 'I have to agree, it makes a lot of sense.'

'I knew you'd probably think so, and it makes it easier, knowing that you understand,' George said.

'How soon were you thinking of leaving?'

'As soon as possible.' George toyed with the papers on his desk. 'No sense hanging around now that the decision is made. I'm aware it may cause a few practical problems here, which is why I also took another decision.' He looked at Paula. 'I know you've only been with us for a few weeks, but you've settled in well. I'd like you to consider staying on, joining the practice, on a permanent basis.'

'Stay on?' Paula gasped. 'But. . .' Dear heaven, did he know what he was asking? She flung a look in Adam's direction. He had turned away and was staring studiously out of the window.

'It was only a suggestion,' George was saying. 'I think you could handle the job. You've had time to get to know us.'

Oh, yes, that was certainly true. If only she could see Adam's face, know what was going on in his mind. Paula ran a hand through her hair. 'I'm flattered by the offer, George.' She gave a half smile. 'I. . .I'd like to think about it, if that's all right?'

Adam turned to look at her, his head raised, his eyes narrowed. George was on his feet. 'I don't need an answer for a few days. After that, obviously, depending on what you decide, the practice will need to start looking for a new partner.'

'Of course—I appreciate that.' Paula nodded. 'I promise you'll have my answer within forty-eight hours.'

'Well, in that case I shall leave you to it and hope you come to the right decision,' George smiled. 'And now I must be on my way—Margaret and I have a few plans to discuss. I imagine the two of you will have things to talk about too.'

The door closed, and Paula found herself the subject of Adam's intense scrutiny. His eyes were dark as he looked at her.

'Does your decision really need such careful consideration?'

'I happen to think it does. After all, it would require a big commitment on my part—something I wasn't prepared for.' She turned away, only to have him take hold of her arm, forcing her to look at him.

'I didn't realise you had other plans,' he said hardly.

'I don't,' she said sharply. 'It isn't that.'

'Then what? Perhaps you don't fancy wasting your professional skills on an average sort of town.'

'It has nothing to do with that!' Her voice seemed to have acquired a defensive squeak. How could she tell him the truth, that to stay, to have to see him every day, work with him, would be like rubbing salt into an open wound? 'I. . .it's a big step, something I hadn't even considered.'

'So what have you to lose?' he persisted. 'You could do a lot worse. You're popular with the patients. If it's a question of where to live, the cottage is yours, for as long as you need it.'

Dammit, did he have to make things more difficult? Paula closed her eyes in a feeble and totally unsuccessful attempt to shut him out of her thoughts. She might have known it wouldn't work. How could it, when he only had to be near her for the wild impulses to start racing up and down her spine?

She jerked her eyes open, deciding that flippancy made a safer refuge. 'You'd better watch out, I might begin to think you actually want me to stay!'

His reaction took her completely unawares. 'It's your decision,' he said raggedly. 'I have no right to influence you one way or the other.'

But he *was* influencing her, she felt like shouting. Whether he knew it or not, she was influenced by him, even though it seemed that he found it easy to stay coolly distant.

She stepped back, telling herself that if she was to think at all rationally she would do it a whole lot better out of his arms.

Taking a deep breath, she forced a smile. 'I'll think about it,' she reiterated. 'Forty-eight hours won't make all that much difference, and if I decide against staying you'll still have time to find a replacement.'

'Paula!'

She hesitated at the door.

'Have dinner with me.'

She stifled a sigh. He was not making things easy. On the other hand, he was right, what had she to lose? 'I'd like that. When?'

'My place, day after tomorrow.'

'Fine.' They could toast her decision—or not, as the case might be.

Time had a habit of not standing still. Forty-eight hours was certainly ample enough for any determined person to make any kind of decision, Paula chided herself. And she had certainly been nothing if not determined. Twenty-four hours ago her decision had been clear-cut; she would turn George's offer down. Twelve hours later the edges of her reasoning had become blurred again.

It was no good, she had to try to be rational about this—put aside any personal feelings, weigh up the pros and cons. On a purely professional basis she couldn't be anything but flattered by George's suggestion that she join the partnership. It must mean that he was confident she could do the job. *She* was confident she could do it. So what was the problem?

Paula sighed. Whichever way she looked at it, she was the loser. If she stayed it would mean working with Adam every day, seeing him with Katy, knowing that he still loved Alison. On the other hand, if she were to leave there were an awful lot of people she would miss. George, Bill, Louise, the baby. . .

'Dammit,' she muttered, 'why keep looking for excuses? At least be honest with yourself. You want to stay.' But how did Adam feel about it?

By the end of the day she had shuffled the thoughts around so much that her head ached. 'A fine evening this is going to be,' she told herself. 'You're a nervous wreck before you even get there. You'd better calm down, start the way you mean to go on.'

Having showered, washed her hair and brushed the chestnut waves until it shone, Paula went through the contents of her wardrobe, and felt the nervousness she had been fighting all day well up with new intensity. She couldn't imagine what had possessed her to agree to have dinner with Adam, especially dinner alone at his house. At least a restaurant would have been neutral ground and far safer. But it was too late to back out now.

She decided finally to wear a simple but elegant

fitted black dress with a scooped neckline and matching short jacket. Jewelled clips in her ears and at her throat added a touch of sparkle.

She was applying her lipstick when the phone rang. Could it be Adam cancelling for some reason? Paula was totally unprepared for the sense of disappointment that washed illogically over her as she snatched up the receiver. She felt almost relieved to hear the voice of Sergeant Davis.

'Dr Fairley? Sorry to have to call you out, but we've had an RTA and need a duty police surgeon. I called Dr Patterson, but he was already out on a call, and I'm afraid this is pretty urgent.'

Paula's response was instantly all professional. 'Give me what details you have, Sergeant.'

'It's a multiple pile-up—a nasty one. A car in collision with a chemical tanker. Three other vehicles are involved.'

'Oh, no!'

''Fraid so. We've raised the emergency services, fire and ambulances, and alerted the local hospital, but so far we haven't been able to free the driver of the first car. From the sound of things I'd say his chances are pretty slim. We've got one fatality so far, three passengers seriously injured. The tanker driver seems to have come off lightest. He's on his way to hospital now.'

'I'll be with you as fast as I can.' Paula replaced the phone, automatically reaching for her bag, then, after a moment's hesitation, picked up the phone and dialled. She heard it ringing and felt her heart turn over as Adam's voice answered, sounding so close that she almost shivered. There was a hint of tension in his voice.

'Paula? Is something wrong?'

'Not exactly.' She glanced at her watch.

'You're not about to cancel and leave me with a mountain of food?'

'No, it's not that. I thought I'd better warn you, I may be late. Something's come up. It occurred to me that you might prefer to cancel.'

'Is it trouble?' he asked sharply.

'Nothing I can't handle. I've had an emergency call from the police. There's been a pile-up, several cars involved, and they're having trouble getting at one of the drivers.'

'I thought Bill was on emergency cover.'

'He is, but he's already dealing with another call. I just thought. . .if you wanted to call things off. . .'

'There's no question of it,' Adam said hardly. 'Paula, give me the details, and I'll meet you there.'

She stiffened. This was one job where she needed all her wits about her. 'That won't be necessary. I'm reserve duty police surgeon; I can deal with it. Besides,' she forced a laugh, 'you don't get out of doing the cooking that easily!'

'Paula. . .'

'I have to go. I'll see you later.' She put the phone down quickly before she could be tempted to change her mind, and sped out to her car.

It was dark by the time she reached the accident

spot, to find emergency floodlights trained on to the jumble of wreckage that had once been several cars.

Grabbing the mac she always kept in the car, Paula went towards the police officer, picking her way over twisted metal as she did so, and found her feet sliding on a layer of foam.

'Sergeant? I got the call. I'm Dr Fairley, duty police surgeon.'

'Glad to see you, Doctor—I'm Sergeant Warwick. We've got a nasty one here.' The sergeant led her towards the vehicles centred in the spotlights. 'We've managed to start getting some of the other cars shifted. By some miracle a couple of the drivers and some passengers weren't too seriously injured. We've managed to get them all ferried to the local hospital. But the tanker is a problem. The first car went straight into him. From the evidence we've managed to get so far, the driver had no chance to avoid him.'

Paula's horrified gaze took in the impacted wreckage of a small car. It seemed to be wedged beneath the body of the tanker. 'My God, what sort of state is the driver in?'

'He's alive, just about. One of our men managed to reach him and was pretty sure there was a pulse.'

Paula drew a deep breath and coughed. 'Chemicals.'

'That's the second problem,' Tony Warwick confirmed grimly. 'There's a leak. The fire brigade have doused everything down, but we want him out of there, fast. Trouble is the door's jammed. We may have to cut in through the roof.'

'In that case the sooner you get me in there the better.'

The young sergeant looked at her. 'You realise it's risky and there's not much room?'

'It goes with the job.' Paula flashed him a wry smile. 'Pretty much like yours. I'm going to need some more direct light. If someone's got a torch, I'll have to make an examination before I can judge how best he should be moved. Perhaps someone could hang on to my case.' She flipped it open and took out a stethoscope. 'He's probably going to need a painkilling injection before you'll be able to move him.'

'Here's a torch, Doc.' A young police constable stepped forward. 'How about if I get up there with you and hang on to it—the case too?'

Paula looked at the constable. 'You don't have to, you know. This is my job.'

He grinned. 'And mine's looking after the public. Besides, I'd rather be doing something. The name's Ken Palmer, by the way.'

'We'd better get to it, then, Ken.' She glanced at the sergeant. 'I'll give you the signal when it's safe to start cutting him out.'

'The rescue crew are standing by.'

'Fine.' She gazed ruefully at her high-heeled shoes and sheer tights. 'Here goes, then.'

She was glad of Ken Palmer's steadying hand as she manoeuvred round the shattered bodywork of the car. Its bonnet was wedged firmly beneath the rear of the tanker. In the dark it wasn't an easy task to get into a position where she could see the man inside, and she was conscious all the time of the lingering smell of chemicals.

'Shine the torch in through here.' Paula indicated the broken window. 'I can see the driver, but he seems to be slumped over to the other side.'

'Probably from the impact,' Ken said softly, his voice surprisingly and comfortingly close. 'I'm surprised there's anything left.'

'I can't. . .reach.' Carefully Paula pulled fragments of broken glass out of the shattered window, wincing as one caught her arm.

'You OK?'

'Yes, fine.' She gritted her teeth. 'Ah, now, bring the torch closer if you can.' The thin flare of light wavered. 'That's right, hold it there.'

'Have you got him?'

'Yes. . .wait, I'll see if I can reach him to get a pulse. He's not looking too good. Damn this light, and the cold.' It had started to rain. She pressed her numbed fingers against the man's neck. 'I can't feel anything, but my hands are pretty well frozen.' Her foot slipped and she cursed softly under her breath. 'Can you pass me the stethoscope? Right, I'll have to lean in through the window. OK, now let's see.' She managed to tug the man's coat aside, and as she did so his head drooped to the side.

For the first time she saw his features clearly in the light from the torch. His grey hair was matted with blood. He must have been around sixty. She applied the stethoscope to his chest, willing herself to find a heartbeat. One look at his face had told her it was already too late, but she clung to a fragment of hope; besides, professionally, she had to satisfy herself that there was no mistake.

'Are you OK, Doc?'

Paula stepped back, easing herself to the ground, coiling the stethoscope as she did so.

'Can you give him something for the pain, Doc?' Ken held her arm, steadying her as she moved back.

'There's nothing I can do,' she said flatly. 'He's dead. I'm only guessing, but I'd say he probably had a massive heart attack. You'll need a post-mortem to confirm it. He probably didn't know anything about the crash.'

The constable's hand shook as he lowered the torch. 'Poor devil!'

Paula glanced at him. 'Are you all right?'

'What? Oh, sure.'

'Take a few deep breaths—it helps,' she advised gently. 'I'd better go and let the sergeant know so that he can make a start on getting this lot shifted.' She made her way over the debris to where the sergeant was talking to the fire officer. 'You can move him whenever you like. 'I'm afraid he's dead—probably a heart attack. There's certainly no evidence of any alcohol.' She sighed, suddenly very weary. 'I'll put in a full report. I'm only sorry I couldn't do more.'

'Thanks a lot anyway, Doc. I'm sorry we had to drag you out.'

'It's all part of the job. Sooner mine than yours.' Raising a hand, she went back to her car and sat for several minutes, gazing back at the scene before starting up the engine and driving away. It wasn't often she indulged in self-pity, but, right now, she felt both useless and depressed.

Adam opened the door at the same instant that she reached it, almost as if he had been waiting for the sound of her car on the drive. He looked tired, and there were deep furrows on his brow as his eyes seemed to blaze at her for an instant, then he drew her inside.

'You look as if you could do with a drink.' He poured brandy, handing her the glass. 'Here, this will warm you up.'

Warm her up! On an empty stomach and with her head already spinning from tiredness and reaction, it was more likely to put her flat on her back.

'I don't know if this is wise,' she protested weakly.

'It's medicinal. I'm not trying to get you drunk.'

She drank and coughed and her head spun even more. The glass was removed firmly from her grasp and Adam was frowning angrily.

'I heard about the crash on the local radio. You didn't mention anything about a chemical tanker being involved.'

'Didn't I?' Her voice sounded strained. Even

when he was angry there was something disturbingly arousing about him, something almost unreal as he stood with the firelight behind him, dark trousers hugging lean hips, his jaw rigid with tension, his eyes appearing a deeper blue than ever. She let her gaze fall warily. 'I must have forgotten.'

Adam drew a ragged breath as he looked at her for a long moment, then he pulled her roughly towards him. 'Have you any idea what I've been going through, waiting, knowing the kind of risks you were taking?' he rasped.

His anger confused her. It seemed illogical in that it implied a feeling she knew didn't exist, unless he believed that she had somehow usurped his own authority.

Colour darkened her cheeks. 'I was simply doing my job. Sometimes risks happen to be a part of it—we all know that.'

'I don't want you taking those risks,' he bit out.

Anger flared. 'Are you saying I'm incapable of doing my job?'

Suddenly it hit her that they were arguing, and she couldn't understand why. Fighting with Adam was the last thing she wanted. She was exhausted, a man had died and she hadn't been able to do a thing to save him, and she was supposed to make decisions about her future. What did he think she was? Inhuman? For a brief moment, as tears welled up, she closed her eyes, only to open them again as his hands tightened on her arms.

'Damn it, don't you understand?' he bit out,

pulling her towards him. 'I don't want anything to happen to you. I don't want to live with the fear, each time you go out, that I might not see you again.' He sighed heavily. 'I'm not putting this very well. God knows, I hadn't planned on any of this happening.'

Paula swallowed hard, her eyes wide. 'I think. . .you'll have to be more specific,' she said frustratedly. 'I'm not sure just what it is that you're trying to say.'

He drew a harsh breath. 'Right now I don't even know if I'm capable of putting it into words.' He touched her cheek. The effect was more potent even than the brandy. She wondered if he was aware of it, then, blushing, realised he must be as his hand moved to caress the curve of her breast, surprising the taut nipple as it flowered in instant response to his touch.

'Paula,' he groaned softly as his mouth made feathering advances over her throat, chin, lips, her eyes, back to her mouth, claiming it with a fierce possession that left them both breathless.

She responded with a ferocity that matched his own, measure for measure. His mouth left hers as he stroked her hair.

'Have you any idea how much I need you?' he choked. 'How much I want you to be a part of my life?'

She raised herself to reach his mouth. 'I want you too—I thought it must be obvious.' She broke off with a moan as he kissed her again. But it was more than want. The sensations he was creating seemed to flood through her, setting off a train of tiny explosions, offering promises but never bringing the fulfilment she craved.

She could feel the heat of his body through the thin sweatshirt, heard her own tiny cry of protest as it seemed to create a barrier between them. Her hands moved jerkily in an attempt to remove it, finally making contact with the smooth silkiness of his skin. 'I love you,' she whispered.

She felt him tense and wanted to weep as his mouth freed hers. She wasn't even aware of having spoken the words aloud until he looked down at her, his breathing uneven, his eyes narrowed.

'I didn't intend this to happen,' he said in self-disgust.

'You. . .you didn't intend making love to me?'

'You must know I have no regrets about that.'

'Then what. . .?' She stared at him in confusion until dull realisation began to dawn. 'Alison,' she murmured thickly. 'How could I have forgotten? How could I have thought. . .?' She saw him frown, then his hand held her chin, forcing her to look up at him.

'What are you saying?' His eyes narrowed. 'What does Alison have to do with any of this?'

Paula sighed. 'I would have thought that was fairly obvious.' She tried to free herself from his grasp, but his hold merely tightened. His expression darkened.

'It may be obvious to you,' he said.

'Can't we just leave it?' she said dully.

'No, we can't.' He frowned down at her. 'You'll have to explain.'

She swallowed hard. 'I understand how you still feel about her, that no one could ever take her place.'

'Paula. . .' He frowned in puzzlement. 'Are you saying. . .? Do you honestly believe I could feel as I do, respond to you as I do, if I still loved Alison?' he asked slowly.

She looked up at him uncertainly. 'I. . .I don't know. I imagine some men could.'

'I'm not *some* men.'

'Then I don't understand.' She blushed. 'If you want me. . .'

'Which I do.' Adam stared down at her.

'Then why?' She drew a deep breath and saw him frown.

'Alison walked out of my life, but she left something behind, don't you see?'

'You mean Katy?'

His mouth tightened. 'Katy is part of me, part of my life, not some separate entity.'

'Anyone looking at her would see that for themselves. But I don't see why that should be a problem.'

A nerve pulsed in his jaw, then he drew her slowly towards him. 'I think maybe I've been a fool.'

'Oh, I wouldn't go as far as that.' She sighed,

relaxing against him. 'But you still haven't explained.'

'It seemed clear-cut to me. I love you, but I'm still not free.' His voice grated. 'How could I expect anyone to take on a ready-made family? What right do I have. . .?'

Paula tilted her head back to look up at him, her fingers brushing against his lips, silencing the words. 'Did it never occur to you that your problem doesn't exist except in your own mind?'

'Not until now,' he replied softly. 'I really have been a fool.'

'A little pig-headed, maybe.' Any other adjectives she might have thought of were stifled as he took possession of her mouth again.

She sighed, fretfully, when Adam raised his head to look down at her with glittering eyes.

'I think you'd better come and eat,' he murmured huskily, 'before I forget why you're here and this gets out of hand.'

Paula swallowed hard. 'I think I just lost my appetite for food.'

'Don't get ahead of yourself,' he chuckled. 'Besides, my powers of self-control aren't limitless.' He sobered then. 'I have no intention of rushing things. Now, let's eat.'

She hadn't imagined she would be hungry, but when it came to it she found she was, in fact, ravenous. Confronted by a huge steak and salad, accompanied by a superb red wine, followed by the lightest of cheesecakes, she ate enthusiastically. In no time at all, it seemed, her plate was clean, and she sat back, amazed at the speed at which the food had disappeared.

'I must have been hungry after all,' she confessed, slightly shamefacedly.

Adam chuckled, pouring more wine. 'I like to watch someone who appreciates their food.'

'You haven't exactly done justice to yours.' She looked at his own hardly touched plate.

'I had other, far more interesting things on my mind.' He was leaning forward, and she could smell the subtle, musky undertones of his aftershave. The whole effect of his nearness was creating an intensity of sexual awareness she had never known before.

'Such as?' she murmured.

'Such as the future—*our* future, for one. We should drink to it if we do nothing else, for tonight at least,' he said softly.

Paula sipped at her refilled glass, then set it down again. 'I think I've had more than enough alcohol for one night. I can hardly think straight.'

'You're sure it's the alcohol?'

She couldn't be sure. It had never had quite this effect before.

Adam drew her to her feet, his gaze holding hers. 'I'll make some coffee in a minute. Right now I'm not sure I can bear to let you go.' His hands had long since removed her jacket and were moving over her body, rousing her again. She closed her eyes, moaning softly.

'I'm not sure this is a good idea. I'm still a working woman. I need some sleep if I'm going to instil any kind of confidence in my patients in the morning.'

He laughed throatily. 'Do we see George together, or would you prefer to see him alone?'

'George?' she murmured breathlessly.

'To let him know that you'll be accepting his offer.' Adam nibbled at her ear.

'I hadn't actually made my decision,' she said weakly.

'Perhaps you need a little more persuading.' He raised his head to look at her, desire still flaring in his eyes. 'You're a good doctor, Paula. I know your work is important to you and the patients need you.' His mouth moved teasingly over hers. 'As long as you have time for my needs as well.'

She groaned as he slid the straps of her dress down. 'Will there be enough hours in the day?'

'We'll make the most of those we do have, and at least I shall know I can stop worrying about you.'

She rocked on her feet, her senses still drugged as she looked up at him. 'Why should you worry about me?'

His mouth tightened. 'I don't ever again intend going through the kind of hell I went through tonight, waiting for you, knowing the sort of risks you were taking.'

A tiny alarm bell started to ring somewhere in her head, so faintly that she hardly registered it. 'I thought we'd settled all that. It's part of the job. I go where I'm needed.'

'But it doesn't have to be.'

Involuntarily she stiffened. 'Aren't you forgetting something? It works both ways. You take risks—we all do. Am I supposed to sit quietly at home, worrying about you?'

'That's different.'

'How is it different?' Paula tensed, waiting for his response. What was happening? Why did she suddenly feel a gulf opening up between them?

Adam's eyes narrowed. 'I would have thought that was obvious.'

'Not to me,' she said, detaching herself slowly from his arms. 'I thought we were talking about an equal relationship, about respecting each other's individuality as well as needs.'

'Paula, you're making too much of this.'

'No,' she said flatly, 'I don't think I am. These are things that need to be said, *now*.' Colour heightened her cheeks. 'More to the point. . .' she sighed heavily '. . .what makes you feel you have the right to apply any kind of pressure where my work is concerned?'

She saw the shock register in his eyes. 'I thought you'd given me that right, the right to love you, not to a division of the spoils,' he rasped harshly. 'Obviously I misread the signals.'

'It seems we both did.' He had mentioned want and need. He hadn't, now she reflected on it, mentioned marriage. She swallowed on the sudden aching tightness in her throat.

Adam frowned. She suspected that, for the first time in his life, he didn't know what to say. 'Is it so wrong of me not to want you to take risks?' he demanded. 'I don't think I can settle for anything less.'

But wasn't he asking her to take the biggest risk of all? A relationship without the ultimate commitment. He might tell himself he no longer loved Alison, but how could she be sure?

Paula sighed as she reached for her bag. 'There's a simple answer. We'd better keep things to a strictly business relationship. That way neither of us gets hurt.'

But the damage, as far as she was concerned, was already done. Adam had taken her to the brink, had even allowed her a glimpse of the exquisite pleasure his lovemaking could hold. But that was as far as his commitment went. She would have to accept him on his terms, and she wasn't sure she could do that, not if to do so meant sharing him with another woman, even one who no longer played any active part in his life.

CHAPTER TWELVE

'I'M DELIGHTED for you,' Paula told Bill as he was on his way out of her consulting-room about a week later. 'I take it Louise has adjusted to the idea of becoming a mother?'

'Adjusted? She's like a broody hen. She's actually knitting!'

Paula laughed. 'It can happen. Give her my love, and remind her that I shall expect to see her at the antenatal clinic.'

'You'd have trouble keeping her away. Come to think of it,' Bill mused, 'I may go along to one of those expectant father meetings. It's never too soon to start picking up a few useful tips.'

Paula gave a wry smile. 'I can see the pair of you are going to become unbearable! Oh, by the way, you may be pleased to hear that Mrs Lucas has entered an official complaint against her husband. I've been asked to give evidence on her behalf.'

'Well, thank God for that.' Bill turned away, and Paula was about to close the door when Adam appeared in the corridor that linked each individual consulting-room.

He looked tired; more than that, he looked drained. His mouth was tight, his blue eyes hard. Paula looked at him sharply. It was a week since she had seen him, and the change in him shocked her.

On the point of quietly closing the door, she felt something hold her back. It wasn't as if she knew what to say. The only thing she was certain of was that she had felt the distance between them as painfully as if it were a tangible thing. At first she had tried to ignore, it, but that wasn't easy, not when she found herself awake in the early hours of each morning, and the doubts came crowding in. Had she made a terrible mistake? Was he going through the same kind of anguish, the soul-searching?

She gave him a remote smile and turned away.

'Paula, I need to talk to you.'

She hovered in the doorway, looking at him warily. Her emotions were so close to the surface that she wasn't sure she could trust herself to be near him without letting go. 'Is something wrong?' she asked hesitantly.

He frowned, dragging a hand through his hair. 'I'm not sure,' he said flatly. 'It's Katy.'

Paula came out to meet him now. 'What do you mean?' Isn't she at school?'

'That's the trouble.' He shook his head. 'She was complaining of a sore throat, so I decided she'd better stay at home today. Annie took her over to stay with her.'

So that was it; he was concerned because Katy had a sore throat. 'Well, you probably made the right decision,' she said woodenly. 'It's always better to be safe than sorry. I'm sure you'll find she's better in the morning.' She had half turned away again when he stopped her.

'Paula, I got a call from Annie about half an hour ago. Katy seems to have disappeared.'

She felt the blood draining from her face as she stared at him. 'What do you mean, disappeared? How can she simply have vanished? There must be a mistake. She's probably hiding somewhere and forgot the time.'

Adam's voice was taut. 'When Annie last saw her she was playing in the garden. Next time she looked, Katy had gone. Annie's almost hysterical, and that's not like her.'

'No, I'm sure it's not,' Paula stammered. 'What has she done so far to find her?'

'That's the thing—she's hunted everywhere, in all the obvious places. The neighbours have joined in.' He drew a harsh breath as he looked at her. 'There's no sign of Katy. It's as if she'd vanished off the face of the earth.'

Instinctively Paula reached out her hand. It was immediately covered by his. 'She. . .she may have gone to visit a friend.'

Adam shook his head. 'I already thought of that. I've spent the past half-hour ringing round. Most of them are at school. I've spoken to the parents of those who aren't. Nothing. No one has seen Katy or heard from her.'

Paula knew the colour had drained from her face.

She lifted her chin, facing him directly. 'I'm sure she'll be all right.'

He gave her one quick look. 'God, I hope so. I'll never forgive myself if anything has happened. . .'

'It won't,' she said firmly. 'She's probably playing quite happily somewhere. Children often tend to find themselves secret little hideaways. She probably got involved in some game and has no idea of the time.' She broke off as an idea struck her. 'What about the cottage? She may have gone there. It's possible.'

'That's what I'm counting on.' He looked down at her. 'She liked being near you. She often talks about you. I don't know why I didn't think of it before. It would be the obvious place for her to go.'

'I'm coming with you.' Paula was already following as he strode away. His hand briefly squeezed her arm.

The drive to the cottage seemed interminable, conscious as she was of Adam's nearness, all the pent-up emotions she sensed were seething through him as he drove. She shared every moment of his anguish. If she could have done anything to lessen it she would have done it, but there was nothing either of them could do to banish the nightmare except wait and pray.

He was driving too fast, though neither of them noticed until the car hit a rut on the uneven road. Paula gasped as she was flung sideways, and Adam dragged his gaze from the road to look at her, his jaw tensing as he deliberately slowed the car.

'Are you all right?' There was a hint of self-disgust in his voice.

Paula swallowed hard. 'I'm fine. Don't worry about me. I'm as anxious to find Katy as you are.'

His expression darkened as he forced his concentration back to the road. 'I *do* worry about you. I never stop worrying about you, or thinking about you.' His voice faltered as he saw the confusion in her eyes. 'If it's any consolation, I haven't had a second's peace of mind since I let you walk out that night.'

She had to force herself to speak through the tightness in her throat. 'I don't recall it being a case of your *letting* me walk out,' she said shakily. 'I seem to remember it was my decision. One I've. . .I've been regretting ever since.' She could feel the pulse hammering in her throat as he swung his gaze back to her.

'Are you saying what I think you're saying?' he asked huskily.

'I think I'm saying that. . .maybe I was too busy considering my own needs to think about anyone else's,' she murmured brokenly.

His breathing was uneven as he glanced down at her before turning his gaze back to the road. 'And just what are your needs?'

She blushed and her nails dug into the palms of her hands. 'I suppose what it comes down to is that I'd rather be with you on any terms than be without you, and Katy, on mine. If that makes any kind of sense.'

His foot seemed to jerk spasmodically on the brake and he swore savagely. 'What do you mean by any terms?' he prompted softly, his eyes narrowed and searching.

'I would have thought that was obvious. I realise that you'll always love Alison, but—well, I've decided it doesn't matter. I couldn't. . .wouldn't even try to take her place.' Paula broke off as he swore savagely.

'What gave you the idea that I still love Alison?' he bit out. 'I'm beginning to doubt that I ever did.' He frowned. 'In fact, though neither of us appreciated it at the time, walking out was probably the only act of kindness Alison ever did in her life.'

'But you. . .I don't. . .'

His mouth tightened grimly. 'My only regret is that in some way Katy got the idea that she was to blame. But as for love,' he scorned, 'Alison didn't know the meaning of the word, and, while I may have been young enough and naïve enough, once, to believe that that was what I felt for her,' his voice gentled as he looked down at her, 'I realise now that it had nothing to do with what I now recognise as love—real love, that is.'

Paula stared up at him, her green eyes wide with confusion.

'We have a lot of talking to do,' Adam grated, 'and I intend to see to it that we do talk, as soon as Katy is found and I know she's safe.'

The car swung to a halt and Paula realised, with a sense of shock, that they were at the cottage. It looked deserted, and her spirits fell as she began, numbly, to climb out of the car. Adam's hand briefly stayed her.

'I mean it, Paula. There are a lot of things we need to get sorted out. We've wasted enough time as it is. I don't intend to waste any more.'

She nodded, breathing shallowly. 'Let's find Katy, then everything will be all right.'

But the cottage was deserted, as she had guessed, deep down, that it must be, since she had the only key and all the doors were securely locked. Together they searched the small garden and the field beyond, calling Katy's name.

The sun was going down and the light beginning to fade when they finally admitted defeat, standing in chilled silence, feeling the worst kind of nightmare beginning to gather and take shape.

'I'd better phone Annie. She may have some news.'

Paula waited as he made the call. She made coffee, her movements automatic as she tried to convince herself that Katy would have been found and the drama over. One look at Adam's face, however, as he came into the kitchen confirmed her worst fears.

'There's still no sign of her. The search parties are still out.' He ground his fist savagely. 'She has to be somewhere. A child of that age couldn't go far. Katy wouldn't, unless——'

'Don't!' Paula's voice contained quiet authority. 'Katy may be young, but she isn't stupid. She wouldn't go far from home and the people she knows.'

'So where is she?' Adam's faced was haggard. 'She must be hungry or thirsty by now. No game would keep her occupied for so long.'

'That rather depends.' Paula tried to speak positively. 'I seem to remember that when I was Katy's age I could become completely engrossed for hours, especially. . .' She broke off.

'What is it?' Adam gripped her arms. 'You've thought of something?'

'Yes, but it's only a guess.'

'We've tried everything else,' he rasped. 'I trust your intuition. Tell me!'

'The kittens.' She stared up at him and saw him frown. 'Don't you see? Katy is fascinated by them. You know how desperately she'd like to have one. Where are they?'

Adam tensed. 'They're in Annie's barn.' A flicker of hope lit in his eyes and faded again. 'But they've already searched it.'

Paula felt like weeping with disappointment, then, '*Where* in the barn?'

'I don't know,' he snapped impatiently. 'On the bales of——'

On the bales of hay. 'Oh, my God, she could be trapped or hurt!'

It took only minutes to reach the farm. Annie Lambert was in the yard as the car screeched to a halt and they ran towards her.

'The barn!' Adam directed.

'But we've already searched——'

'I'm going to look again. Paula thinks she could have been playing with the kittens.'

Adam flung the heavy doors open. They stood, the three of them, listening, breathing hard. Total silence. Adam's face tightened grimly.

'We'll start searching again. She could be hurt, unconscious.'

Paula flung herself at the bales, tearing them aside as if they weighed nothing, praying she would find what they were looking for and that everything would be all right. A child could climb into the smallest space, hiding perhaps, thinking it was a game, becoming trapped.

Her mouth was dry as she hunted feverishly, refusing to abandon hope. Every instinct was telling her that Katy was here, somewhere.

She called out, 'Katy, where are you? If you can hear me, shout, darling!' She wasn't sure whose must be the greatest terror, hers or Katy's or Adam's as he worked, grim-faced.

And then she heard it, the faint mewling of a kitten. For a moment she froze, stock-still, listening. She must have imagined it. But no, there it was again, and there too was the tiny bundle of fur, struggling to crawl from beneath a fallen bale. And then another sound, faintly, this time no animal but a child—a frightened child.

With a strength she didn't even know she possessed Paula dragged at the bales. Somehow a hollow must have been formed as several had slipped and now lay at angles, leaving just enough space for a child. Then she saw it, the tiny flash of colour. Blue, a dress, and a child's voice, calling plaintively.

'Adam!' Paula screamed as loud as her lungs would allow, at the same time she was manoeuvring carefully, terrified of bringing the weight crashing down. 'I've found her! She's here, but I can't move the bales.'

Somehow the bale shifted and with a little cry Katy reached for her, her pale little face, eyes large with tears as she flung herself at Paula.

'I was playing with the kitten,' she sobbed. 'It crawled into the hole and I climbed in too, then it moved and I got stuck!'

'I know, darling, I know. But it's all right now.' Paula hugged the small figure, the little wet face next to her own.

Adam was beside them, his breathing harsh and uneven as he put his arms round them both.

'She's all right,' Paula murmured, revelling in the loving warmth of him. She could feel his heart beating beneath his shirt. 'She's frightened, probably very hungry.' The words were for Annie Lambert's comfort as much as for Adam's as she saw the white-faced young woman watching.

'I'll never forgive myself, never!' sobbed Annie.

'It wasn't your fault. Katy went into the barn after one of the kittens.'

'Those damned kittens!'

Adam winced. 'They do seem to have been

responsible for a certain amount of chaos. Unfortunately I suspect that an awful lot of the blame also lies with me.' He held Paula's gaze. 'Right now I'm going to take these two ladies home.'

Katy buried her head deeper against Paula's neck. 'You won't go, will you? I don't want you to go.'

Paula looked up at Adam, her eyes glistening with tears. 'I don't. . .'

'Let's go home,' he rasped. 'We'll give Katy a bath and something to eat. After that we have some talking to do.'

An hour later, looking none the worse for her adventure, Katy was asleep with one tiny black kitten curled up on the counterpane beside her.

'I'm not sure this is encouraging good habits,' Adam breathed as they finally both moved away and he closed the bedroom door quietly.

'She'll grow out of it,' Paula promised. 'And even if she doesn't—well, I can think of far worse things that could happen.'

Downstairs neither of them made any move to light the lamps. The glow from the fire was enough, enclosing them both in its warm circle.

Suddenly Paula felt very shy, which was ridiculous when she loved this man so much that just to be near him made her legs feel weak. Perhaps it was the way he was looking down at her, with a kind of lazy intent that seemed to strip her naked, drawing her into his own warmth. And it wasn't entirely imagination.

'Paula?' Adam's arm tightened round her shoulders as he drew her towards him. She heard his sharp intake of breath as she relaxed against him, her head against his chest. 'I don't think I shall ever be able to let you go again.'

'And I'm not sure I'd want you to.'

He cupped her chin, looking down at her tenderly, but still with a hint of the anguish he had been through in his eyes. 'When I think of how close I came to losing both of you——'

'Don't!' Her fingers brushed against his mouth, silencing the words.

He shook his head, taking her hand in his. 'I want you to know about Alison.'

'You don't have to tell me. It isn't important.'

'I want to tell you. I don't want there to be anything between us, ever.' His mouth twisted. 'My love for Alison died long before she finally left us. I'm not saying it was her fault. I couldn't always be there when she wanted. After a while she began to stay on at parties after I had to leave. I didn't mind; there was no reason why she should miss out simply because of my work. But then she started going out alone. Sometimes. . .sometimes she didn't come home. Or I'd get back to find she'd left Katy with a baby-sitter.'

Paula gave an involuntary shudder. 'But at least you have Katy.'

'Oh, yes,' he said tightly. 'Thank God we had

Katy before Alison decided that having a child didn't quite fit in with her plans or the kind of life she was beginning to discover a liking for.'

Confusion briefly clouded Paula's eyes. 'But the cottage? You lived there.'

He nodded. 'For a while, until Alison decided it wasn't large enough. We bought this house.' He gave a light, humourless laugh. 'Six months later she walked out. She'd met someone else, an American, the president of some company, whatever. He could afford to keep her in the manner to which she had every intention of becoming accustomed.' His hand smoothed the silky softness of her cheek.

'But at least you didn't have to fight her for Katy.'

'I would have done. She knew it. And a child would have been an encumbrance. What I can't forgive her for is that she left without explaining why. For a long time Katy blamed herself, thought it was something she'd done.'

'But she understands now.'

He nodded. 'I think at last she's beginning to.'

'But you didn't move back to the cottage,' she said softly, made drowsy by the warmth of the fire and the joyful knowledge that she was in his arms.

'I couldn't go back. I tried. For the same reason that I may have seemed reluctant to sell it.' His hand moved against her hair, caressing her cheek. 'It held too many bad memories—the constant arguments—and Katy could never go there without somehow associating it with her mother leaving, even though she was tiny when all this happened.'

'Children are very aware of atmosphere. They also have far greater intelligence than people give them credit for.'

He turned her face up to his. 'Yet she came to you there. I wonder why, if she only associated it with bad things.'

'Curiosity, perhaps?' she murmured.

He gave a short laugh. 'Curiosity and cats do seem to go together—or, in this case, kittens.' His mouth came down on hers, gently at first, then becoming more demanding until they broke apart, breathlessly. 'I made up my mind that work and Katy were enough, that I didn't need anything or anyone else in my life. I like my work.'

'So do I.' Paula stared up at him earnestly.

'I realise that. I was being selfish when I thought I could place restrictions on it.'

'Maybe I over-reacted. It's something we have to come to terms with. The risks will always be there, but we have each other.'

His lips moved against hers. 'You'll definitely be staying, then, Dr Fairley?'

'Oh, yes, I think so, Dr Sinclair.'

'You realise I'm asking you to take on more than a job? Marriage is also part of the deal.'

She gazed up at him. 'You strike a hard bargain. I may have to think about it.'

He kissed her, and this time he was more

demanding. 'You've had enough time,' he rasped as he broke away.

'In that case, I accept.' Paula smiled up at him dreamily.

'Just think. . .' he held her tightly in his arms. '. . .the three of us together.'

'Four,' Paula murmured.

'Four?'

She nodded. 'You forgot the kitten.'

She closed her eyes tightly as their kiss sealed the bargain, and when she opened them again, much later, it was to see Katy standing in the doorway, clutching the kitten, smiling knowingly!

Family Practice
Only One Cure

ASSOCIATION OF MAIL ORDER PUBLISHERS
mps
MAILING PREFERENCE SERVICE